Thomas Anderson

Florula Adenensis

A systematic account, with descriptions, of the flowering plants hitherto

found at Aden

Thomas Anderson

Florula Adenensis
A systematic account, with descriptions, of the flowering plants hitherto found at Aden

ISBN/EAN: 9783337381912

Printed in Europe, USA, Canada, Australia, Japan

Cover: Foto ©Andreas Hilbeck / pixelio.de

More available books at **www.hansebooks.com**

JOURNAL

OF

THE PROCEEDINGS

OF

THE LINNEAN SOCIETY.

SUPPLEMENT TO VOL. V.—BOTANY.

FLORULA ADENENSIS.

A SYSTEMATIC ACCOUNT, WITH DESCRIPTIONS, OF

THE FLOWERING PLANTS HITHERTO FOUND AT

ADEN.

By THOMAS ANDERSON, Esq., M.D., F.L.S.,
H.M.'s Bengal Medical Service.

LONDON:
LONGMAN, GREEN, LONGMANS AND ROBERTS,
AND
WILLIAMS AND NORGATE.
1860.

SUPPLEMENT

TO THE

JOURNAL OF THE PROCEEDINGS

OF THE

LINNEAN SOCIETY OF LONDON.

Florula Adenensis. A systematic Account, with Descriptions, of the Flowering Plants hitherto found at Aden. By Thomas Anderson, Esq., M.D., F.L.S., H.M.'s Bengal Medical Service:

[Read November 1, 1860.]

Much attention has of late years been directed to the military station of Aden, owing to its rapidly increasing importance, both in a political and commercial point of view; and now that it is visited weekly by the large steamers in their course to India, China, and Australia, its name has become as familiar as that of any of our Eastern settlements. From its commanding position at the entrance to the Red Sea, and from its forming an indispensable link in the chain of communication with our Eastern Empire, the importance of the settlement will increase with the development of our Indian possessions.

Besides the interest attaching to Aden as an isolated stronghold of Britain, and as the probable starting-point whence European civilization will spread over the rich territory of Arabia Felix, its physical peculiarities have always attracted considerable attention ; and the anomalous appearance of its rugged, barren pinnacles of rock leaves an indelible impression on the memory of its numerous visitors, while a closer examination of its narrow valleys, and of the steep cliffs that almost encircle them, discloses a strange, though scanty, assemblage of plants and insects. Indeed, so striking is its flora, that the Arabs, the original possessors of Aden, ages ago appropriated to the rock the Arabic name of its most peculiar and beautiful flower*.

Since Salt, who visited Aden in 1809, and probably collected a few plants there, several botanists, on their way to more productive regions, have spent a few hours in exploring its more accessible gorges during the detention of the steamer for a supply of coals. In 1846 M. P. Edgeworth, Esq., of the Bengal Civil Service, a gentleman well known by his valuable memoirs on Indian Botany and his long-continued labours in the cause of that science in India, collected 42 species within a very circumscribed area; the result of which limited botanical excursion was communicated to the Asiatic Society of Bengal in 1847. The insurmountable difficulties attending the identification of such obscure species as those composing the Aden flora, without having access to extensive libraries and herbaria, are shown by the alterations I have made in many of the specific names proposed by Mr. Edgeworth; while at the same time his valuable suggestions and accurate descriptions prove his extensive knowledge of genera and species. Fortunately for our knowledge of the flora, Dr. J. D. Hooker, on his route to India in 1847, remained two days at Aden, and made a most extensive and nearly complete collection of its plants.

On his return to England in 1851, with the assistance of Dr. T. Thomson, his fellow-traveller, he largely increased the number of specimens of his previous collection, and also added some species to the list. Lieut.-Colonel Madden and Sir Robert Schomburgk have also contributed a few species from Aden among their general collections sent to Sir W. Hooker. While detained at Aden on my return from India in May 1859, I was enabled to make two short excursions nearly to the centre of the peninsula, and, considering the limited character of the flora, I secured an extensive set of specimens of nearly all its species. I was so fortunate as to find most in a good state for identification; the result of a copious fall of rain which had occurred about three weeks before my visit, and which had brought most of the plants into flower, and imparted a slight tint of green to many of the least sterile

---

* "Aden" is the Arabic name of that beautiful and remarkable shrub the *Adenium obesum* (*Nerium obesum*, Forsk.). The European residents consider the species as quite peculiar to Aden; but this is an error, as it is found on some of the rocky promontories along the coast of the Red Sea. The name *Adenium*, adopted by Roemer and Schultz for this and another species (*A. Hongel*), is merely the Arabic name Latinized.

valleys. From these materials the present Florula has been compiled.

Most of the plants have required a careful comparison with a large suite of specimens from various localities, and the consultation of a formidable array of works on Indian and Arabian botany, in order to determine their synonymy and geographical distribution.

These labours have been greatly lightened by daily reference to Sir William Hooker's unrivalled herbarium and rich library; of both of which I have been permitted to make unrestricted use. Without repeated examinations of the East Indian Herbarium, and of the Arabian, Abyssinian, and Egyptian collections of Sieber, Delile, Aucher-Eloy, Schimper, and other travellers, in all of which the Kew Herbarium is peculiarly rich, the work could not have been accomplished. To Dr. Hooker I am indebted for hourly advice and assistance ; while his entire Aden collections have been placed at my disposal for examination and description. Without this privilege the Florula could not have been commenced, as his collections considerably exceeded my own in number of species, and they thus form the basis of the Flora. To G. Bentham, Esq. I have to acknowledge my obligations for assistance in the determination of several specimens of *Leguminosæ, Scrophularineæ,* and *Lavandula*; as well as for the free use of his Herbarium.

Before proceeding to the purely descriptive matter, it appears desirable to notice, 1st, the physical aspect and climate of Aden ; 2nd, a few of the peculiarities of its flora ; 3rd, some facts in the geographical distribution of the species ; and finally, to institute a comparison between its flora and those of one or two similarly situated localities.

1. Aden is a small rocky peninsula, in many features resembling our other stronghold, Gibraltar ; and is situated on the southern coast of Arabia, in 12° 47' N. lat., and 45° 10' E. long. The maritime region called Tehama, of which it is a promontory, is a sandy, barren tract from 20 to 100 miles in breadth, extending along the shore of the Red Sea, from a point a little east of Aden to the Gulf of Akaba. A mountainous region of 4–7000 feet in elevation rises immediately beyond ; this, from its height, attracts a considerable portion of the moisture borne from the Indian Ocean by the north-west monsoon, and thus, enjoying a climate favourable to the growth of luxuriant cereals and fruits, it has for ages been called the Happy Arabia. It forms a striking contrast to the sterile Tehama, in the southern portion of which rain but rarely

falls, while towards its northern extremity it is quite unknown. The few streams that enter from the mountains of Arabia Felix are speedily lost in its arid sands ; cultivation is therefore confined to the vicinity of the few towns and villages, and is dependent on a precarious supply of water from wells. The area of the Aden peninsula is about fifteen miles, its greatest breadth being five miles and its least three. It is connected with the Arabian coast by a narrow sandy isthmus, covered at high spring-tides ; but formerly it was probably an island, since the whole district is of recent origin, being evidently a raised sea-beach ; as is shown by the remains, twenty-three miles inland, of the ancient seaport of Mooza, formerly frequented by the Phœnicians. The peninsula is entirely composed of volcanic rocks of apparently great age, forming numerous precipitous peaks and narrow ridges, which on the southern and eastern sides rise from the sea in inaccessible cliffs, attaining their greatest elevation, 1775 feet, in the peak " Jibeel Shumshum." On the eastern side and towards the isthmus is a considerable depression, the crater of the volcano, surrounded on nearly all sides by high walls of rock and cinder. From the serrated ridge Jibeel Shumshum, numerous narrow valleys, shut in by precipices, radiate on all sides towards the sea, in which some end abruptly, while on the northern side others widen out into the limited sea-beach.

The only patches of vegetation occur at the base of these gorges, just above the sea-line ; and the loose and tolerably fertile soil accumulated there consists of scoriæ mixed with sand and the detritus washed from the rocks above by the violent torrents which rush down every ravine after the rare but heavy falls of rain. Along the cliffs utter sterility reigns, except where a ledge of rock or a mass of cinder has allowed the accumulation of sufficient earth to afford sustenance to a few straggling bushes of *Capparis galeata* or *Adenium obesum*.

In so low a latitude the sun shines with intense force nearly throughout the year, and at Aden the solar power is increased by every peculiarity of physical conformation and climate. The undisturbed atmosphere stagnates in the walled-in valleys, where a death-like stillness always reigns. The black and naked rocks absorb by day the scorching rays transmitted through an ever-cloudless sky, only to radiate the pent-up heat by night, thus confining to the shore the cool but feeble breezes that occasionally spring up from the Indian Ocean. Accordingly, even in December, when the sun's power is at its lowest, Dr. Hooker found the

temperature of the soil at 107° Fahr. a few feet below the surface. In the hotter seasons of the year, the sun, even in the early
morning, is overpowering, and above the rocks the air flickers
from the intense heat; while all distant objects are distorted by an
imperfect mirage. Almost perpetual drought is, of necessity, the
concomitant of such a climate as I have described, and accordingly
the annual rain-fall at Aden never exceeds 6 or 7 inches; this
scanty amount being spread over the period between October and
the end of April; while occasionally none falls for a year and a
half. Still Aden is not considered unhealthy, even to Europeans,
who seem to become soon accustomed to the heat; and so great is
our power of adaptation to circumstances, that after a residence
of a year or two the climate is spoken of as cool and pleasant from
October to the end of March, and as bearable during the remain-
der of the year.

2. The vegetation of Aden closely resembles that of Arabia
Petræa, of which it is evidently the southern extension. It is
eminently of a desert character; the species being few in number
(only 94), and being quite disproportioned to the number of
genera and Natural Orders; even when the flora is compared
with those of localities having similar areas, and similar rela-
tions to the mainland. Most of the species are limited in the
number of individuals, a few only of the more arid forms pre-
dominating. *Dipterygium glaucum*, six or seven species of *Capparidaceæ*, *Reseda amblyocarpa*, *Cassia pubescens* and *obovata*,
Acacia eburnea and a few *Euphorbiaceæ* are the only common
plants; and some of these are so plentiful, that in many places
they abound to the exclusion of all other plants. The other
species are either very local, or sparingly scattered over the
peninsula.

All the species are more or less peculiar in their habit, and
some are so strange in their appearance as to constitute the ano-
malies of the Natural Orders to which they belong. As examples
may be enumerated:—*Sphærocoma Hookeri* among *Caryophyllaceæ*,
Adenium obesum, with its almost globular fleshy trunk, naked
branchlets bearing a tuft of leaves and an umbel of beautiful
flowers, *Moringa aptera*, in which the leaves are reduced to long
subrigid raches, the prickly *Jatropha spinosa*, and, strangest of all,
the *Æluropus Arabicus*, a grass with short spiny leaves, so sharp,
that it was with the greatest difficulty I could procure specimens
of it. The bright-green colour, which forms so pleasing a feature
of the vegetation of the temperate and moist tropical regions of

the globe, is quite unknown at Aden.   Here foliage is reduced to
a minimum, and the superfluous moisture given off by leaves in less
arid climates is stored up in fleshy stems against seasons of long-
continued drought.   With the exception of some *Capparidaceæ*
and *Reseda amblyocarpa*, all the plants have either glaucous
whitened stems and leaves, or are completely covered with a hoary
pubescence.

Aridity, while reducing the amount of cellular tissue, has also
favoured the production of spines; and though in many cases
the development has not attained actual spinosity, still in rigid
or distorted branches and asperities of stem and leaf bears witness
to the modifying influence of the climate.   Of the ninety-four
species that constitute the flora, sixteen bear sharp thorns on some
part of their structure.   In some the leaves terminate in sharp,
recurved hooks; in others the stipules are spinous; in a few the
bracts are prickly, and in *Lycium europæum* and *Euphorbia cuneata*,
the short stiff branches are terminated by short thorns.   Several
species yield gums or resinous matter, and their stems frequently
become encrusted by these exudations, probably caused by the
bark cracking from exposure to the great heat of the sun.   I have
observed resinous substances accumulated in various quantities on
Balsamodendron opabolsamum, Acacia Edgeworthii, Adenium obesum,
and the shrubby *Euphorbiæ*.   All the *Capparidaceæ* (with the
exception of *Mærua Thomsoni*), *Dipterygium glaucum*, *Reseda amblyocarpa*, the *Compositæ*, and a few others, are characterized by
more or less pungency or aromatic odour,—qualities always pos-
sessed by plants of desert regions.

The small proportion of species to the number of genera and
Natural Orders will be perceived by an examination of the accompanying Table :—

	Genera.	Species.		Genera.	Species.
Cruciferæ	3	3	Moringeæ	1	1
Capparidaceæ	4	9	Leguminosæ	8	11
Resedaceæ	1	1	Cucurbitaceæ	2	2
Polygalaceæ	1	1	Portulacaceæ	2	2
Caryophyllaceæ	2	2	Umbelliferæ	1	1
Malvaceæ	2	3	Rubiaceæ	1	1
Sterculiaceæ	1	1	Compositæ	5	5
Tiliaceæ	2	2	Apocyneæ	1	1
Geraniaceæ	1	1	Asclepiadaceæ	2	2
Zygophyllaceæ	2	2	Convolvulaceæ	2	3
Rhamnaceæ	1	1	Boragineæ	1	1
Terebinthaceæ	1	1	Solanaceæ	1	1

	Genera.	Species.		Genera.	Species.
Scrophularineæ	4	4	Paronychiaceæ	1	1
Acanthaceæ	1	1	Nyctagineæ	1	2
Verbenaceæ	1	1	Euphorbiaceæ	3	7
Labiatæ	1	1	Urticaceæ	1	1
Plumbagineæ	1	1	Gnetaceæ	1	1
Salvadoraceæ	1	1	Amaryllideæ	1	1
Phytolaccaceæ	1	1	Cyperaceæ	1	1
Salsolaceæ	1	1	Gramineæ	9	9
Amarantaceæ	2	2			

Total number of natural orders, 41; of genera, 79; of species, 94.

This aggregation, within so considerable an area, of almost solitary representatives of genera, is probably a feature peculiar to isolated desert localities. It first attracted my attention during my visit to Aden in 1859, and I have since drawn up tables of the species, genera, and natural orders of the Floras of Hong-Kong, Ischia, and Gibraltar; the results of which confirm my first impression. Hong-Kong and Ischia are nearly equal to Aden in area, and, though differing from it in being detached from the mainland, the sea has proved a less insurmountable barrier to the introduction of species from the neighbouring countries than the unpropitious climate of Aden, and the inaccessible walls of rock by which it is cut off from the rest of Arabia. Gibraltar, though of smaller extent than Aden, yet possesses so many features in common with it, as fully to justify a comparison of their floras. I am indebted to Mr. Bentham for the materials from which the Table of the Hong-Kong species is deduced. That of the flora of Ischia is taken from Gussone's elaborate Florula of that island*, all the cultivated and doubtful species and genera having been carefully rejected. Kelaart's 'Flora Calpensis' is the authority for the list of species of Gibraltar.

Table showing the proportion of Natural Orders, Genera, and Species in the Floras of Aden, Hong-Kong, Ischia, and Gibraltar.

	Natural Orders.	Genera.	Species.
Aden	1	1·92	2·29
Hong-Kong	1	4·59	7·90
Ischia..............	1	4·32	9·23
Gibraltar	1	3·50	6·70

The actual paucity of species in the vegetation of Aden, though indicated by this Table, will be more distinctly seen by a reference to the numbers from which the proportions were obtained.

* 'Enumeratio Plantarum Vascularum Inarimensium.'

	Natural Orders.	Genera.	Species.
Aden	41	79	94
Hong-Kong	122	560	965
Ischia	86	372	794
Gibraltar	68	243	456

These tables show that the great preponderance of natural orders and genera, relatively to the number of species, is not necessarily a distinguishing mark of the vegetation of similar localities; since it is not the result of situation or isolation, but is entirely due to climatic causes. In regions favourable to vegetation, as in Hong-Kong, Ischia, and Gibraltar, the balance is preserved by a constant struggle for existence going on between the species. At Aden, however, no such struggle takes place; but all the species have to strive against conditions tending to the entire extinction of vegetable life. Viewed in this light, the Flora appears a collection of desert species, selected from widely different natural orders and genera, and all alike contending with the excessive heat and drought.

Before noticing some facts in the geographical distribution of the species, I have only to advert to the unequal proportion borne by monocotyledonous to dicotyledonous plants. But eleven out of the ninety-four species are monocotyledons, of which nine are grasses. Of the remaining two, one is an exceedingly rare plant at Aden (*Pancratium tortuosum*), of which I found a solitary clump. The entire absence of Palms and *Polygonaceæ* seems also worthy of record. In so dry a climate Ferns and other Cryptogamia, with the exception of Lichens, are quite unknown.

3. The geographical distribution of even so small a number of species possesses several points of interest, particularly when regarded with reference to the extension of the Arabic Flora over the arid regions of the earth. Of the ninety-four species composing the Florula, fourteen, or a little less than a sixth, are endemic, and one constitutes a new genus, confined to Aden. They are as follows :—

Cleome paradoxa, *R. Br.*
—— pruinosa, *T. Anders.*
Mærua Thomsoni, *T. Anders.*
Sphærocoma Hookeri, *T. Anders.*
Hibiscus Welshii, *T. Anders.*
Sterculia Arabica, *T. Anders.*
Tavernieria glauca, *Edgew.*
Acacia Edgeworthii, *T. Anders.*
Ptychotis Arabica, *T. Anders.*
Convolvulus sericophyllus, *T.Anders.*
Anarrhinum pedicellatum, *T.Anders.*
Campylanthus junceus, *Edgew.*
Lavandula setifera, *T. Anders.*
Euphorbia systyla, *Edgew.*

The remaining eighty species have an extensive geographical

.listribution, fourteen occurring over all the barren parts of the globe. The following Table shows how they spread east and west from Arabia as their centre :—

Table of Distribution of Aden Plants.

	Species.		Species.
Arabia	68	North-west India ...	21
Scinde	44	Persia	19
Egypt	29	Senegal	19
Abyssinia	25	Mediterranean	18

The desert flora, of which these species form a part, attains its greatest breadth in the African desert, about 5° east longitude, where it covers the territory between the 10th and 37th degrees of north latitude. In Asia, though prolonged into Scinde and the western portion of the Punjab, it is diminished in breadth to 7° or 8° of latitude; its southern limit being 23° north latitude in Scinde, and 30° or 31° north latitude in Affghanistan and the Punjab. The limits of this vegetation may be defined as follows:—Starting from its head-quarters, the rainless region of Arabia, the flora extends over the peninsula of Arabia, with the exception of the south-western mountainous district, and along the shores of the Persian Gulf, whence it spreads into Southern Persia. It includes the whole of Beloochistan, South Affghanistan, Scinde, and a part of the Punjab. West from Arabia Petræa the flora passes into Egypt and Nubia, and partially into Abyssinia, and extends over the African desert to Senegal; finding its western limit in the Cape de Verd Islands. Even there it retains many of its most desert types, as is shown by the flora of these islands containing twenty-nine genera common also to Aden and other parts of Arabia, and eleven species absolutely identical : a resemblance the more remarkable from the small number of species composing the Cape de Verd Flora. Webb, in the 'Spicilegia Gorgonica,' enumerates only 235 species of flowering plants, of which the following genera are represented at Aden. Those plants of which the specific name is given are identical in both floras.

Polygala triflora, *Linn.*
Mollugo.
Abutilon.
Corchorus Antichorus, *Roem.*
Grewia.
Fagonia cretica, *Linn.*
Zygophyllum simplex, *Linn.*
Zizyphus.

Indigofera.
Rhynchosia.
Cassia.
Acacia.
Citrullus colocynthis, *Schrad.*
Oldenlandia.
Vernonia.
Heliotropium.

Campylanthus.
Lavandula.
Statice.
Ærua Javanica.
Boerhaavia scandens, *Linn*.
Euphorbia.
Forskohlea.

Cyperus.
Tricholæna Teneriffæ, *Parlat*.
Panicum viride, *Linn*.
Pennisetum cenchroides, *Rich*.
Aristida Adscensionis, *Linn*.
Eragrostis ciliaris, *Link*.

[Read 21st June 1860.]

CONSPECTUS GENERUM FLORULÆ ADENENSIS.

Classis I. *DICOTYLEDONES*.

Subclassis I. Thalamifloræ.

Ordo I. CRUCIFERÆ.

Tribus I. ALYSSINEÆ.   *Silicula bivalvis, septo lato.*

1. FARSETIA, *Turra*.   *Calyx* clausus.   *Stamina* tetradynama ; filamentis edentulis.   *Silicula* lineari-oblonga ; valvis planis ; septo venoso uninervio.   *Semina* plura, marginata.

Tribus II. ISATIDEÆ.   *Silicula indehiscens.*

2. DIPTERYGIUM, *Decaisne*.   *Corollæ* petala integra.   *Stamina* tetradynama ; filamentis edentulis.   *Silicula* latere compressa, crustacea, dorso utrinque alata, unilocularis, monosperma.

Tribus III. BRASSICEÆ.   *Siliqua septo lineari.*

3. DIPLOTAXIS, *DC*.   *Calyx* patens.   *Stamina* tetradynama.   *Siliqua* elongato-linearis, compressa ; valvis uninerviis, membranaceis.   *Stylus* conicus, brevissimus.   *Semina* ovata, biseriata.

Ordo II. CAPPARIDACEÆ.

Tribus I. CLEOMEÆ.   *Fructus capsularis.*

1. CLEOME, *Linn*.   *Stamina* 4–6, toro subgloboso inserta.   *Stylus* brevissimus.   *Capsula* siliquæformis, unilocularis, bivalvis ; valvis deciduis, a septo seminifero solutis.

Tribus II. CAPPAREÆ.   *Fructus baccatus.*

2. CADABA, *Forsk*.   *Sepala* 4, biseriatim valvata.   *Corollæ* petala

4 vel nulla. *Stamina* 4–5, apici tori stipiformis inserta. *Appendix* tubulosa, linguæformis, a basi tori exserens. *Ovarium* longe stipitatum. *Bacca* siliquæformis, subtorulosa.

3. CAPPARIS, *Linn.* *Sepala* 4, in æstivatione imbricata. *Corollæ* petala 4. *Stamina* indefinita, toro parvo hemisphærico inserta. *Ovarium* stipitatum. *Bacca* globosa. *Semina* plurima, in pulpa immersa.

4. MÆRUA, *Forsk.* *Calyx* infundibuliformis ; tubo persistente, limbi lobis æstivatione valvatis, deciduis. *Corolla* nulla. *Stamina* plurima. *Bacca* siliquæformis, valde torulosa.

Ordo III. RESEDACEÆ.

1. RESEDA, *Linn.* *Calyx* 6-partitus. *Petala* 5. *Stamina* 10–30. *Carpidia* 3. *Capsula* obovata, apice hians.

Ordo IV. POLYGALACEÆ.

1. POLYGALA, *Linn.* *Sepala* 5, duo lateralia (alis) latiora, petaloidea. *Corolla* irregularis, petala inferiore carinata. *Stamina* 8, monadelpha. *Capsula* membranacea, obovata, compressa, monosperma.

Ordo V. CARYOPHYLLACEÆ.

1. MOLLUGO, *Linn.* *Calyx* 5-partitus. *Petala* nulla. *Stamina* 5. *Stigmata* 3, linearia. *Capsula* trilocularis, obtuse trigona, loculicide trivalvis. *Semina* plurima.

2. SPHÆROCOMA, *T. Anders.* *Calyx* 5-partitus, persistens. *Petala* 5, subhypogyna. *Stamina* 5. *Ovarium* uniloculare, biovulatum. *Stylus* solitarius; stigmate bifido. *Utriculus* chartaceus, abortu monospermus.

Ordo VI. MALVACEÆ.

Tribus I. HIBISCEÆ. *Calyx involucello cinctus.*

1. HIBISCUS, *Linn.* *Involucellum* 5–10-phyllum. *Calyx* 5-fidus. *Petala* 5, in æstivatione convoluta. *Tubus stamineus* columnæformis. *Ovarium* sessile, 5-loculare. *Semina* lanata vel sericea.

Tribus II. SIDEÆ.   *Calyx involucello nullo, nudus.*

2. ABUTILON, *Gärtn.*   *Involucellum* nullum.   *Ovarium* 8–10-loculare.   *Cocca* trisperma.

Ordo VII. STERCULIACEÆ.

1. STERCULIA, *Linn.* *Flores* unisexuales. *Calyx* coloratus, campanulatus. *Corolla* nulla.   *Tubus stamineus* solidus, apice 10-lobatus. *Ovarium* stipitatum, carpellis 5.   *Follicula* 4. *Semina* pauca.

Ordo VIII. TILIACEÆ.

1. CORCHORUS, *Linn.* *Sepala* 4, decidua. *Petala* 4, unguiculata. *Stamina* 8–10. *Capsula* quadrilocularis, quadrivalvis, polysperma.

2. GREWIA, *Linn.* *Calyx* pentaphyllus. *Corollæ* petala 5, basi intus glandula vel foveola nectarifera instructa. *Stamina* plurima, apici stipitis brevis inserta. *Ovarium* quadriloculare. *Drupa* quadriloba, tetrapyrena.

Ordo IX. GERANIACEÆ.

1. ERODIUM, *L'Hér.* *Calyx* 5-partitus. *Petala* 5, caduca. *Stamina* 10, monadelpha, biseriata; 5 fertilia, 5 ananthera vel obsoleta, basi glandulis instructa. *Styli* 5, gynophoro longitudinaliter adnati. *Carpella* 5, abortu monosperma; stylis a gynophoro elastice et spiraliter solutis.

Ordo X. ZYGOPHYLLACEÆ.

1. FAGONIA, *Tourn.* *Calyx* 5-partitus, deciduus. *Petala* 5, calyce longiora. *Stamina* 5, æqualia. *Capsula* pyramidalis, pentagona, pentacocca.

2. ZYGOPHYLLUM, *Linn.* *Calyx* 5-partitus, deciduus. *Petala* 5, emarginata, calyce paulo longiora. *Stamina* 10, corolla breviora; filamentis subulatis, flexuosis; antheris ovatis. *Capsula* ovata, pentagona, 5-locularis.

Subclassis II. **Calycifloræ.**

Ordo XI. RHAMNACEÆ.

1. ZIZYPHUS, *Tourn.* *Calyx* patens, 5-fidus. *Petala* 5, calycis

fauci inserta. *Discus* planus. *Stamina* 5, petalis opposita. *Ovarium* biloculare, in disco immersum. *Ovula* solitaria, erecta. *Styli* 2. *Fructus* carnosus. *Semina* erecta, compressa.

Ordo XII. TEREBINTHACEÆ.

1. BALSAMODENDRON, *Kunth*. *Flores* polygami. *Calyx* 4-dentatus, persistens. *Petala* 4, sub toro inserta, æstivatione valvatim induplicata. *Stamina* 8, cum petalis inserta. *Ovarium* biloculare. *Ovula* in loculis gemina. *Drupa* abortu sæpissime unilocularis, monosperma.

Ordo XIII. MORINGEÆ.

1. MORINGA, *Juss*. *Calyx* 5-partitus. *Petala* 5, duo longiora, æstivatione imbricata. *Stamina* 8–10, disco cupuliformi inserta; filamentis basi liberis, supra medium connatis, apice distinctis. *Ovarium* uniloculare; placentis parietalibus 3. *Fructus* leguminiformis, rostratus, torulosus, trivalvatus; valvis dissepimenta transversa gerentibus. *Semina* uniseriata, trigona.

Ordo XIV. LEGUMINOSÆ.

Subordo PAPILIONACEÆ.

Tribus I. LOTEÆ.

† Subtribus *Genisteæ*.

1. ARGYROLOBIUM, *Eck et Zey*. *Calyx* bilabiatus; labio superiore bi-, inferiore tridentato. *Vexillum* semiorbiculatum; *alæ* oblongæ; *carina* obtusa. *Stamina* monadelpha. *Legumen* lineari-ensiforme, subcompressum, utrinque acutum, stylo apiculatum, 6–10-spermum. *Flores* flavi.

†† Subtribus *Indigoferæ*.

2. INDIGOFERA, *Linn*. *Calyx* urceolato-campanulatus, 5-fidus. *Vexillum* subrotundatum, reflexum; *alæ* oblongæ, carinam æquantes; *carina* obtusa, gibba, basi utrinque calcarata. *Stamina* diadelpha. *Legumen* teretiusculum, oblongum, falcatum, 2–5-spermum. *Flores* coccinei.

††† Subtribus *Galegeæ*.

3. POGONOSTIGMA, *Boiss*. *Calyx* ebracteolatus, subæqualiter 5-

dentatus. *Vexillum* suborbiculatum, carinam alasque superans; *alæ* basi cum carina connexæ; *carina* acuta, incurva.
Stylus incurvus; stigmate capitato, longe barbato. *Ovarium*
biovulatum. *Legumen* ovatum, compressum, monospermum.
Flores purpurei.

4. TEPHROSIA, *Pers.* *Calyx* ebracteolatus, subcampanulatus,
5-fidus, laciniis superioribus profundius fissis. *Vexillum*
suborbiculatum, carinam et alas paulo superans. *Stamina*
10, monadelpha. *Stigma* pubescens. *Legumen* lineare, compressum, rectum. *Semina* 5–12, compressa.

Tribus II. VICIEÆ.

Subtribus *Hedysareæ.*

5. TAVERNIERA, *DC.* *Calyx* bibracteolatus. *Vexillum* sub-
ovatum; *alæ* calyce breviores; *carina* obtusa, vexillum æquans.
Stamina 10, diadelpha. *Stylus* longus, flexuosus, filiformis.
Legumen biarticulatum; articulis compressis, monospermis.
Flores rosei.

Tribus III. PHASEOLEÆ.

Subtribus *Rhynchosieæ.*

6. RHYNCHOSIA, *Lour.* *Calyx* bilabiatus; labio superiore bifido,
inferiore trifido. *Vexillum* obovatum, alas liberas superans;
carina falcata, rostrata. *Stamina* 10, diadelpha. *Legumen*
membranaceum, compressum, falcatum, dispermum. *Semina*
lævia, notata. *Flores* flavi.

Subordo CÆSALPINEÆ.

Tribus CASSIEÆ.

7. CASSIA, *Linn.* *Calyx* pentaphyllus, deciduus. *Petala* 5,
unguiculata, inæqualia. *Stamina* 10, inæqualia; filamentis
liberis. *Legumen* compressum; septis transversis. *Semina*
compressa, verticalia.

Subordo MIMOSEÆ.

Tribus ACACIEÆ.

8. ACACIA, *Neck.* *Flores* polygami, hermaphroditi et masculi.

Corolla tubulosa aut campanulata, limbo 5-fido. *Stamina* numerosa, exserta; filamentis liberis. *Legumen* crassum, pulpa farctum, aut coriaceum, membranaceum, indehiscens vel vix dehiscens.

Ordo XV. CUCURBITACEÆ.

1. CUCUMIS, *Linn.* *Flores* monoici. MASC. *Calyx* campanulatus, 5-dentatus. *Stamina* 5, triadelpha, calyci inserta; antherarum loculis linearibus, infra apicem connectivi crassiusculi simplicis adnatis. FEM. *Calycis* tubus subglobosus; limbo 5-dentato. *Pepo* carnosus, sulcatus, verrucosus.

2. CITRULLUS, *Neck.* *Flores* monoici. MASC. *Calyx* profunde 5-fidus. *Stamina* 5, triadelpha, imæ corollæ inserta; antheris unilocularibus, loculo lineari, connectivi marginem dorsalem gyrose adnato. FEM. *Calycis* tubus globosus; limbo profunde 5-fido. *Pepo* globosus, lævis, carne solida.

Ordo XVI. PORTULACEÆ.

1. TRIANTHEMA, *Linn.* *Calyx* bracteolatus; tubo cum ovario connato; limbo 5-partito, intus colorato. *Corolla* nulla. *Stamina* 5. *Ovarium* uniloculare. *Stigma* abortu unicum, excentricum. *Capsula* subcylindrica, apice truncata, disperma, parte superiore circumscisse dissiliente. *Semina* subreniformia, rugosa.

2. ORYGIA, *Forsk.* *Calyx* 5-partitus, persistens. *Petala* plurima, ovali-oblonga, integerrima, tenerrima, calyce breviora. *Stamina* plurima, calyci inserta, partim cohærentia. *Ovarium* liberum, 5-loculare. *Stigmata* 5. *Capsula* chartacea, quinquevalvis. *Semina* plurima, reniformia, atra.

Ordo XVII. UMBELLIFERÆ.

1. PTYCHOTIS, *Koch.* *Involucrum* oligophyllum. *Calycis limbus* 5-dentatus. *Petala* emarginata, bifida, cum lacinula inflexa. *Fructus* latere compressus, muricatus. *Mericarpia* 5-juga.

Ordo XVIII. RUBIACEÆ.

1. OLDENLANDIA, *Linn.* *Calycis* limbus 4-dentatus, dentibus in fructu erectis. *Corolla* tubulosa; limbo subrotato. *Capsula* subglobosa, apice rimula loculicide operta. *Semina* plurima.

b

Ordo XIX. COMPOSITÆ.

Subordo TUBULIFLORÆ. *Flores hermaphroditi. Corolla regularis.*

Tribus I. VERNONIACEÆ. *Capitula multiflora, homogama, discoidea. Antheræ ecaudatæ. Flores cyano-purpurei.*

1. VERNONIA, *Schreb. Involucrum* imbricatum, floribus brevius. *Receptaculum* nudum. *Corollæ* limbus 5-fidus. *Achenia* callo basilari cartilagineo. *Pappus* biserialis; series exterior paleacea; interior aristæformis, multo longior.

Tribus II. ASTEROIDEÆ. *Capitula multiflora, homogama. Antheræ basi caudatæ. Flores lutei.*

2. VARTHEMIA, *DC. Involucrum* imbricatum, squamis adpressis acutis. *Receptaculum* alveolatum. *Corolla* tubulosa. *Achenia* oblonga, compressa, pubescentia. *Pappus* biserialis.

3. IPHIONA, *DC. Involucrum* imbricatum; squamis adpressis, acuminatis, mucronatis. *Receptaculum* alveolatum. *Corollæ* tubus nullus. *Achenia* subcylindrica, sulcata, sparse hispida. *Pappus* rigidus, multiserialis; setis intimis corollam æquantibus.

4. HOCHSTETTERIA, *DC. Involucri* squamæ pluriseriales, subæquales, lineari-lanceolatæ. *Receptaculum* hirsutum. *Corolla* tubulosa. *Achenia* subturbinata, villosa; villis achenium superantibus. *Pappus* uniserialis; setis 10, dense ciliatis.

Subordo LIGULIFLORÆ. *Flores hermaphroditi, ligulati. Capitula pauciflora. Flores lutei.*

5. BRACHYRAMPHUS, *DC. Involucrum* imbricatum; squamis acuminatis, margine scariosis. *Receptaculum* nudum. *Corolla* ligulata. *Achenia* oblonga, muricata, breviter rostrata. *Pappus* pluriserialis, pilosus, mollis, albus.

Subclassis III. Corollifloræ.

Ordo XX. APOCYNEÆ.

1. ADENIUM, *Ræm. et Sch. Calyx* 5-partitus. *Corolla* subinfundibuliformis, pubescens, intus lineis 5, villosis longitudi-

ualiter notata. *Stamina* 5, brevissima, inclusa. *Antheræ* cum stigmate cohærentes. *Ovaria* 2, globosa. *Stylus* superne incrassatus; stigmate bidentato. *Succus* lacteus.

Ordo XXI. ASCLEPIADACEÆ.

1. STEINHEILIA, *Decaisne. Calyx* 5-partitus. *Corolla* campanulata, 5-fida; lobis acutis, erectis, contortis; fauce squamulis 5, flavidis, clausa; tubo basi foveolis 5, squamulis alternantibus. *Antheræ* membrana oblonga, stigmati incumbente, terminatæ. *Pollinia* pendula, subcompressa, clavata. *Stigma* muticum.

2. GLOSSONEMA, *Decaisne. Calyx* 5-partitus. *Corolla* subcampanulata, profunde 5-fida; lobis erectis paginaque superiore tuberculo carnoso instructis. *Pollinia* ovoidea, ad apicem funiculo geniculato affixa. *Stigma* 5-gonum. *Folliculus* ovoideus, spinis innocuis echinatus.

Ordo XXII. CONVOLVULACEÆ.

1. CONVOLVULUS, *Linn. Calyx* pentaphyllus. *Corolla* campanulato-infundibuliformis; limbo 5-plicato. *Stamina* 5, imo corollæ tubo inserta, inclusa. *Ovarium* biloculare; loculis biovulatis. *Stylus* unicus; stigmatibus 2. *Capsula* bilocularis, bivalvis. *Semina* 4.

2. CRESSA, *Linn. Calyx* pentaphyllus. *Corolla* infundibuliformis; limbo 5-partito, lobis planis. *Stamina* 5, exserta. *Ovarium* biloculare; loculis biovulatis. *Styli* 2. *Capsula* abortu monosperma.

Ordo XXIII. BORAGINEÆ.

1. HELIOTROPIUM, *Tourn. Calyx* 5-partitus. *Corolla* hypocraterimorpha; fauce nuda; limbo 5-fido. *Stamina* 5, corollæ tubo inserta. *Ovarium* quadriloculare; loculis uniovulatis. *Stylus* terminalis; stigmate peltato.

Ordo XXIV. SOLANACEÆ.

1. LYCIUM, *Linn. Calyx* urceolatus, 5-dentatus. *Corolla* infundibuliformis, tubulosa; limbo 5-fido, erecto. *Stamina* 5, medio corollæ inserta, inclusa. *Ovarium* biloculare. *Stylus* simplex; stigmate capitato, obsolete bilobo. *Bacca* subglo-

bosa, calyce persistente suffulta, bilocularis. *Semina* plurima, reniformia.

Ordo XXV. SCROPHULARINEÆ.

1. ANARRHINUM, *Desf.* *Calyx* profunde 5-partitus. *Corolla* tubulosa; tubo incurvo, basi non calcarato; fauce pervia; limbo bilabiato. *Stamina* 4, didynama, cum rudimento quinti sterilis. *Antheræ* reniformes, uniloculares. *Capsula* bilocularis, chartacea, polysperma; loculis sub apice poro dehiscentibus.

2. ANTICHARIS, *Endl.* *Calyx* 5-partitus. *Corolla* tubulosa; fauce elongata, ampla; limbo 5-fido. *Stamina* 2, antica, inclusa. *Capsula* ovata, subrostrata, bisulca, loculicide bivalvis; valvulis demum fissis. *Columna* placentifera integra.

3. LINDENBERGIA, *Lehm.* *Calyx* campanulatus, semifidus. *Corolla* bilabiata; labio superiore erecto, inferiore trilobo, palato biplicato. *Stamina* 4, fertilia; antherarum loculis disjunctis. *Capsula* ovoidea, bisulca, loculicide bivalvis; valvulis integris. *Columna* placentifera 4-partibilis.

4. CAMPYLANTHUS, *Roth.* *Calyx* 5-partitus. *Corollæ* tubus elongatus, incurvus; limbo patente, subæquali. *Stamina* 2, inclusa; antherarum loculis mucronatis. *Capsula* bilocularis, ovato-compressa, septicide dehiscens.

Ordo XXVI. ACANTHACEÆ.

1. BLEPHARIS, *Pers.* *Calyx* 5-partitus, inæqualis; lacinia infera bidentata. *Corolla* unilabiata; labio 5-fido; fauce cartilaginea. *Stamina* 4; antheris unilocularibus, margine ciliato-barbatis; filamentis inferis supra antheras prolongatis. *Capsula* 4-sperma. *Semina* testa floccosa. *Spicæ* spinosæ, imbricato-bracteatæ.

Ordo XXVII. VERBENACEÆ.

2. BOUCHEA, *Cham.* *Calyx* tubulosus, plicatus. *Corolla* infundibulari-hypocraterimorpha; limbo oblique sub-bilabiato. *Stamina* 4, didynama, inclusa; antherarum loculis oppositis. *Capsula* dicocca, calyce inclusa; coccis elongatis, unilocularibus, multistriatis.

Ordo XXVIII. LABIATÆ.

1. LAVANDULA, *Tourn.* *Calyx* ovato-tubulosus, subæqualiter 5-dentatus, 15-nervius. *Corollæ* tubus exsertus; limbo oblique bilabiato. *Stamina* 4, tubo corollæ inclusa, declinata; filamentis glabris, liberis. *Nuculæ* 4, glabræ. *Flores* in spicis nudis terminalibus.

Ordo XXIX. PLUMBAGINEÆ.

1. STATICE, *Willd.* *Calyx* scariosus, 5-costatus. *Corolla* ima basi tantum gamopetala. *Stamina* 5, petalis opposita. *Styli* 5, staminibus alterni; stigmatibus filiformibus, cylindricis. *Utriculus* unilocularis, monospermus, membranaceus, indehiscens.

Ordo XXX. SALVADORACEÆ.

1. SALVADORA, *Linn.* *Sepala* 4, parva. *Corolla* membranacea, 4-partita. *Stamina* 4, perigyna, corollæ lobis alterna; antheris introrsis, bilocularibus. *Stigma* sessile, simplex. *Bacca* monosperma. *Semen* erectum.

Subclassis IV. **Monochlamydeæ.**

Ordo XXXI. PHYTOLACCEÆ.

1. LIMEUM, *Linn.* *Calyx* profunde 5-partitus, herbaceus, margine membranaceus, laciniis subæqualibus. *Petala* distincta 3-5. *Stamina* 6-7, petalis alterna, disco perigyno inserta; antheris versatilibus. *Ovarium* biloculare. *Styli* 2. *Capsula* dicocca. *Cocci* monospermi, compressi, tuberculati.

Ordo XXXII. SALSOLACEÆ.

1. TRAGANUM, *Del.* *Calyx* 5-fidus, demum crasso-induratus, laciniis apteris. *Corolla* nulla. *Stamina* 5, toro inserta. *Filamenta* crassa. *Torus* (nectarium) inter stamina et pistillum, carnosus, obtuse 5-gonus. *Styli* 2, subulato-filiformes. *Utriculus* depressus, monospermus, indehiscens, calyce reconditus. *Caulis* articulatus. *Folia* succulenta.

Ordo XXXIII. AMARANTACEÆ.

1. ÆRVA, *Forsk.* *Flores* tribracteati, laterales, abortivi nulli. *Perigonium* pentaphyllum, lanatum. *Stamina* 5, basi in cupu-

lam connata. *Antheræ* introrsæ, biloculares. *Staminodia* 5, dentata. *Stylus* subsessilis ; stigma bifidum. *Utriculus* evalvis, monospermus.

2. SALTIA, *R. Br. Flores* tribracteati, abortivi 1–2. *Perigonium* (calyx) pentaphyllum. *Stamina* 5 ; filamentis subulatis compressis, basi in cupulam connatis. *Stylus* simplex ; stigmate capitato globoso. *Ovarium* uniovulatum.

Ordo XXXIV. PARONYCHIACEÆ.

1. COMETES, *Burm. Flores* ternati. *Bracteæ* demum plumoso-pinnatifidæ. *Calyx* herbaceus, 5-partitus ; segmentis spinoso-mucronatis. *Corolla* nulla. *Stamina* 5 ; filamentis subulatis, basi in cupulam subhypogynam connatis. *Staminodia* (petala) 5, linearia, staminibus alternis. *Utriculus* membranaceus, monospermus, indehiscens. *Semen* erectum.

Ordo XXXV. NYCTAGINEÆ.

1. BOERHAAVIA, *Linn. Perigonium* coloratum, tubulosum; limbo plicato, deciduo. *Stamina* 3, subinclusa vel exserta. *Ovarium* uniloculare, uniovulatum. *Stylus* simplex ; stigma obtusum. *Fructus* (achenium) perigonii tubo inclusus, angulato-costatus. *Semen* erectum ; testa cum endocarpio connata.

Ordo XXXVI. EUPHORBIACEÆ.

1. EUPHORBIA, *Linn. Flores* monoici, involucro communi dentato inclusi. *Calyx* et *corolla* nulla. MASC. plures, stamine unico, filamento articulato glandulaque minuta consistentes. FEM. unicus, centralis, longius stipitatus. *Ovarium* triloculare. *Styli* tres, distincti vel plus minus coaliti, bifidi. *Capsula* tricocca ; coccis monospermis.

2. CROZOPHORA, *Neck. Flores* monoici. MASC. *Calyx* 5-partitus, æstivatione valvatus. *Petala* 5, æstivatione convoluta. *Stamina* 8–10 ; filamentis basi coalitis ; antheris extrorsis. FEM. *Calyx* 10-partitus. *Corolla* nulla. *Ovarium* sessile. *Styli* 3, bifidi. *Capsula* tricocca ; coccis monospermis.

3. JATROPHA, *Linn. Flores* monoici. MASC. *Calyx* 5-partitus ; segmentis æstivatione convolutis. *Petala* 5, æstivatione convoluta, cum glandulis 5 alternantia. *Stamina* 8 ; antheris introrsis. FEM. *Calyx* et corolla nulla. *Ovarium* glandulis

(petalis) cinctum. *Styli* 3, distincti. *Stigmata* peltata, undulata. *Capsula* tricicocca; coccis monospermis.

Ordo XXXVII. URTICACEÆ.

1. FORSKOHLIA, *Linn.* *Flores* androgyni, in receptaculo lanato involucro communi cincto. MASC. *Perigonium* monophyllum. *Stamen* unicum; filamentum elastice prosiliens; anthera extrorsa. FEM. *Perigonium* ventricosum, lanatum. *Ovarium* uniloculare, uniovulatum. *Stylus* simplex. *Stigma* lineare, unilaterale.

Ordo XXXVIII. GNETACEÆ.

1. EPHEDRA, *Tourn.* *Flores* dioici; bracteis decussatim oppositis. MASC. *Perigonium* membranaceum, tubulosum, apice bivalve. *Stamen* unicum; anthera bilocularis; loculis apice poro dehiscentibus. FEM. *Perigonium* nullum. *Ovarium* apice pervium, uniloculare, uniovulatum. *Drupa* baccata, monosperma.

Classis II. *MONOCOTYLEDONES.*

Ordo XXXIX. AMARYLLIDEÆ.

1. PANCRATIUM, *Linn.* *Perigonium* superum, infundibuliforme, corollinum; tubo elongato; limbo regulariter 6-partito. *Corona* faucis tubulosa, exserta, dentata. *Stamina* 6, 3 sterilia, in coronam faucis connata. *Ovarium* triloculare, multiovulatum.—*Herbæ* scapigeræ; radice bulbosa.

Ordo XL. CYPERACEÆ.

1. CYPERUS, *Linn.* *Spiculæ* multifloræ, compressæ, terminales umbellatæ; involucro communi 3-4-phyllo; glumis distiche imbricatis. *Glumæ* unifloræ. *Aristæ* hypogynæ, ovarii nullæ. *Stamina* 2-3. *Stylus* trifidus.

Ordo XLI. GRAMINEÆ.

Tribus I. PANICEÆ. *Spiculæ bifloræ.*

1. TRICHOLÆNA, *Schrad.* *Spiculæ* bifloræ, laxe paniculatæ. *Gluma* florifera mutica. *Palea* binervia, obtusa. *Lodiculæ* 2, distinctæ. *Stamina* 3. *Styli* 2; stigmata plumosa.

2. PANICUM, *Linn.* *Spiculæ* subbifloræ, dense spicæformes. *Glumæ* exteriores 3, plerumque vacuæ 4-6-nerviæ. *Gluma*

florifera concava, enervis. *Lodiculæ* 2, carnosæ, truncatæ, obtusæ. *Stamina* 3. *Styli* 2.

3. PENNISETUM, *Pal. de Beauv.* *Spiculæ* bifloræ, in spicas cylindricas, densas, aristatas, confertæ. *Gluma* florifera membranacea, concava, mutica, paleam complectens. *Lodiculæ* 2, fere obsoletæ. *Stamina* 3. *Styli* 2, basi paulo connati.

Tribus II. STIPACEÆ. *Spiculæ uniflora. Gluma florifera aristata. Ovarium stipitatum.*

4. ARISTIDA, *Linn.* *Glumæ* 2, membranaceæ, inæquales. *Gluma* florifera coriacea, teres, involuta, apice aristata; arista trifida. *Palea* membranacea, mutica. *Lodiculæ* 2, integræ. *Stamina* 2. *Styli* 2, distincti.

5. STIPAGROSTIS, *Nees.* *Glumæ* 2, membranaceæ, subæquales. *Gluma* florifera chartacea, membranacea, apice biloba, inter lobos aristata; arista trifida. *Palea* obtusa. *Lodiculæ* 2, spathulato-cochleariformes.

Tribus III. CHLORIDEÆ. *Spiculæ quadrifloræ vel multifloræ. Glumæ et paleæ aristatæ; aristæ tortæ. Ovarium sessile.*

6. TETRAPOGON, *Desf.* *Flores* inferiores 2, hermaphroditi; superiores 2, imperfecti. *Glumæ* 2, carinatæ; superior mutica, inferior aristata. *Gluma* florifera trinervia, carinata, sub apice aristata. *Palea* bicarinata, aristata. *Lodiculæ* 2, integræ.

7. DACTYLOCTENIUM, *Willd.* *Flores* distichi, hermaphroditi. *Glumæ* 2, carinatæ, compressæ; superior aristata, inferiorem complectens. *Gluma* florifera carinata, sub apice mucronata. *Palea* bicarinata. *Lodiculæ* 2, emarginatæ.

Tribus IV. FESTUCEÆ. *Spiculæ multifloræ. Ovarium sessile.*

8. ERAGROSTIS, *Pal. de Beauv.* *Spiculæ* compressæ, paniculatæ. *Gluma* florifera membranacea, trinervia, carinata, decidua. *Palea* bicarinata, persistens; carinis ciliatis. *Caryopsis* libera.

9. ÆLUROPUS, *Trin.* *Spiculæ* compressæ, spicato-racemosæ. *Gluma* florifera coriacea, multinervia, ecarinata, margine membranacea. *Palea* bicarinata.

FLORULA ADENENSIS.

Classis I. DICOTYLEDONES.

Ordo I. CRUCIFERÆ.

1. FARSETIA, *Turra.*

1. F. STYLOSA (*T. Anders.*). Pilis adpressis incana; foliis paucissimis, linearibus, basi attenuatis; sepalis lineari-lanceolatis, margine scariosa, glabra, angusta; siliquis breviter pedunculatis, linearibus, subincanis, stylo apiculatis; stylo 1 lin. longo.—*Mathiola stylosa*, Hochst. et Steud. in Schimper, Pl. Arab. Fel. n. 860.

Hab. Aden, in arenosis (*Hook. fil. et T.!*).

Distr. In deserto Arabiæ Felicis!

Decaisne, in Ann. Sc. Nat. ser. 2. vol. iv. p. 69, describes another species, *F. longisiliqua*, from Yemen, but of which Walpers, in Repert. vol. i. p. 139, says, "Non hujus generis esse videtur." I have not seen this plant. *F. linearis*, Dcne. MSS. in Herb. Mus. and Boiss. in Ann. Sc. Nat. ser. 2. vol. xvii. p. 150, I distinguish from *F. stylosa* by its smaller flowers, ovatelanceolate sepals, and much longer styles. I have seen specimens of it from Muscat and Algiers.

2. DIPTERYGIUM, *Decaisne.*

1. D. GLAUCUM (*Dcne. in Ann. Sc. Nat.* ser. 2, iv. p. 67). Foliis petiolatis, ovatis vel lanceolatis, integris, herbaceis, glabris, vel crassiusculis scabridis; sepalis æqualibus, lanceolatis, obscure trinerviis, extrorsum glandulosis; petalis lanceolatis, obtusis, unguiculatis, sepalis longioribus; stylo tereti, stigmate capitato; ovario sessili, tetraquetro, angulis dentato-alatis; siliculis indehiscentibus, compressis, elliptico-oblongis, scorbiculatis, crustaceo-corrugatis.—*D. scabrum*, Decaisne, fide Boiss. in Auch. Pl. Arab. n. 4150 (absque descriptione). *Pteroloma Arabicum*, Hochst. et Steud. in Schimp. Pl. Arab. Fel. n. 851.

Hab. Aden, a littore usque ad alt. 1000 ped. in monte "Jibeel Shumshum" (*Hook. fil.! T. Anders.*).

Distr. In Arabia Felici! et Petræa! Nubia! Scinde! Punjab!

Herba perennis, subvirgata, glabra vel scabrido-glutinosa, subaphylla.

Ramuli teretes, rigidi, ditfusi. *Folia* 2–10 lin. longa, 1–3 lin. lata. *Sepala* interdum glabra, 1 lin. longa; juniora violacea. *Petala* demum subdeflexa, viridescentia aut alba. *Siliculæ* alis cristatis; duæ laterales majores, duæ antica et postica minores inconspicuæ; uniloculares, abortu monospermæ.

3. DIPLOTAXIS, *DC.*

1. D. PENDULA (*DC. Syst.* vol. ii. p. 630, et *Prod.* i. p. 222). Foliis obovatis, lanceolatis, grosse dentatis, hispidis; sepalis ovatis, tomentosis; siliquis pedicellatis, pendulis, glabris, linearibus, basi attenuatis; stylo brevissimo, stigmate bilabiato.—*d. crassifolia, D. Lagascana, D. hispida* (DC. in Syst. atque Prod. *l. c.*). *D. nana* (Boiss.).
Hab. Aden, in arenosis sterilibus (*Hook. fil.*!).
Distr. In Arabia Felici!' et Petræa, Ægypto! Syria! Persia! Algeria! Hispania! Sicilia!
Herba in hirsutia foliorumque forma multum varians; corolla et siliquis exceptis, plerumque hispida. *Corolla* flava, magna.

Ordo II. CAPPARIDACEÆ.

Tribus I. CLEOMEÆ, *Linn.*

1. CLEOME, *Linn.*

Sect. *Pedicellaria.* Torus carnosus; thecaphorus elongatus.

1. C. PARADOXA (*R. Br. in Salt. Abyss.*; *DC. Prod.* vol. i. p. 241). Caule basi suffruticoso, erecto, glabro, apice glandulis nigris scabro; foliis 3–6-foliolatis; foliolis linearibus, lanceolatis, acutis, mucronatis, glaucis; petiolis foliolis duplo longioribus, muricatis; racemis terminalibus, in fructu elongatis, laxis, subaphyllis; pedunculis thecaphorisque glandulosis, scabris; sepalis ovatis, glandulosis; petalis unilateralibus, apice et marginibus glandulosis, duobus majoribus spathulatis, duobus brevioribus breviter unguiculatis; staminibus 6; stylo brevi, crasso, basi glanduloso; stigmate obtuso; siliquis stipitatis, linearibus, utrinque acutis, glabris, venosis; seminibus biscriatis, glabris, globosis.—*C. muricata,* Edgew. in Journ. Soc. Asiat. Bengal. xvi. p. 1212.
Hab. Aden, ubique in arenosis (*Edgeworth, Hook. fil. et T.*! *Madden*! *T. Anders.*).
Suffrutex perennis, 2–3-pedalis, glaucus, apice glanduloso-scaber, foliosus, ramosus. *Foliola* 1–1½ unc. longa. *Petiolus* foliolo triplo longior. *Flores* magni, flavi. *Siliqua* 4½ lin. longa, pendula; valvis planis 4 lin. latis.

Sect. *Siliquaria.* Torus parvus; thecaphorus brevis vel nullus.

† *Foliis simplicibus.*

2. C. QUINQUENERVIA (*DC. Prod.* i. p. 239). Herbacea, glauca, subpubescens aut glanduloso-hirsuta; foliis longe petiolatis, ovatis, basi
subcordatis, 5-nervibus, floralibus minoribus; floribus axillaribus;
sepalis linearibus, pubescentibus, margine ciliatis; petalis ovatis;
staminibus 6; stylo gracili, glabro; stigmate rotundo, obtuso; siliquis
sessilibus, ovato-oblongis, glanduloso-scabris, stylo brevi apiculatis.
Hab. Aden, in arenosis prope littus (*Madden*!).
Distr. In Persia! Affghanistan!
Herba annua. *Folia* longe petiolata, late ovata. *Siliqua* erecta, 1 unc.
longa, subteres. *Stylus* brevis, 1 lin. longus. *Flores* pallide flavi.

3. C. PRUINOSA (*T. Anders.*). Caule ramosissimo, subglabro; ramis
pruinosis, pilis patentibus subhirsutis, foliosis; foliis petiolatis, ovatis,
acuminatis, trinerviis, papillis scabris sparse hirsutis, marginibus
glandulosis subserratis; floribus axillaribus solitariis; sepalis lanceolatis, subglandulosis; petalis linearibus, unguiculatis; staminibus 4;
siliquis sessilibus, erectis, glandulosis, teretibus, oblongis, stylo persistente deflexo apiculatis.
Hab. Aden, copiossisime (*Hook. fil.*! *T. Anders.*).
Suffrutex parvus, apice glandulosus, sparse pilosus. *Folia* longe petiolata, 4–8 lin. longa, 3–6 lin. lata; petiolus ¾ unc. longus. *Stylus*
gracilis, glaber, 4 lin. longus. *Siliqua* glandulosa, longitudinaliter
sulcata, 8 lin. longa. *Flores* viridi-flavi.

A species very near C. *droseræfolia*, but differing from it in being almost
glabrous, in the shape of the leaves, and in the shorter styles. It may
eventually prove to be a state of C. *droseræfolia*, especially as that plant
has not been found at Aden, though it is common in Arabia Petræa, and
Egypt.

4. C. PAPILLOSA (*Steud. Nomencl.* ed. 2, i. p. 382). Herbacea, gracilis;
caule erecto, pilis patentibus hirsutis; foliis ovatis, basi subcordatis,
margine integro, pilis strigosis papillisque duris scabris, inferioribus
longe petiolatis, superioribus sessilibus; racemis laxis; floribus pedunculis filiformibus; sepalis lanceolatis, glandulosis; petalis lanceolatis,
longe unguiculatis; staminibus 6; siliquis glabris, filiformibus, teretibus, patentibus, pedicello multo longioribus, transversim corrugatis,
rubris; seminibus uniseriatis.—*C. gracilis,* Edgew. in Journ. Soc. Asiat.
Bengal. vol. xvi. p. 1212. *C. linearis,* Stocks, MSS. in Herb. Hook.
Hab. Aden, in locis saxosis (*Edgew., Hook. fil.*! *T. Anders.*).
Distr. In Abyssinia! Scinde! Punjab!
Herba gracilis, annua, aromatica, odore moschato. *Folia* integra.
Corolla junioribus violacea, interdum flava. *Siliqua* glabra, filiformis,
1 unc. longa.

†† *Foliis trifoliolatis.*

5. C. BRACHYCARPA (*Vahl*, ined.; *DC. Prod.* i. p. 240). Caule ramoso, suberecto, glanduloso, apice scabro; foliis 3–5-foliolatis, petiolatis; foliolis ovatis, oblongis; floralibus sessilibus, 3-foliolatis vel integris; floribus laxe racemosis, pedicellatis; sepalis lanceolatis, petalis multo brevioribus, glandulosis; petalis ovatis, unguiculatis, glabris; stamini- bus 6; stylo erecto, glabro, siliqua dimidio breviore; stigmate rotundo; siliquis ovatis, glandulosis, patentibus, demum erectis, stylo capitatis. —*C. Vahliana*, Fresen. Mus. Senckenb. ii. p. 110. *C. diversifolia*, Hochst. et Steud. in Schimp. Pl. Arab. Fel. n. 762. *C. moschata*, Stocks, MSS. in Herb. Hook.

Hab. Aden, in arenosis vulgatissime (*Edgew., Madden, Hook. fil., T. Anders.*).

Herba annua? suberecta, ramis diffusis. *Pedicelli* graciles, siliqua fere duplo longiores. *Flores* flavi.

Tribus II. CAPPARIDEÆ.

2. CADABA, *Forsk.*

1. C. GLANDULOSA (*Forsk. Descr.* p. 68). Foliis subrotundis, ovalibus, mucronatis vel obtusis, crassiusculis, hirsutis, glandulosis; racemis terminalibus paucifloris, floribus pedunculatis; sepalis spathulatis, glandulosis; petalis nullis; staminibus 5, filamentis glabris; toro ligulæformi, petaloideo, staminibus longiore; ovario stipitato, glandu- loso; stigmate sessili; capsulis ovato-oblongis, pedicellatis, glandu- loso-hirsutis.—*Stræmia glandulosa*, Vahl, Symb. vol. i. p. 20. *Ca- daba monopetala*, Edgew. in Journ. Soc. Asiat. Bengal. xvi. p. 1212.

Hab. Aden, in monte " Jibeel Shumshum " dicto, ad altitudinem 1000 ped. (*Edgeworth, Hook. fil. et T.*! *T Anders.*).

Distr. In regione Tehama Arabiæ Felicis.

Frutex apice hirsutus, viscosus, ramosissimus. *Folia* integerrima, petio- lata, 4–10 lin. longa, 3–6 lin. lata, petiolum æquantia. *Flores* apetali. *Capsula* baccata, semipollicaris.

2. C. LONGIFOLIA (*DC. Prod.* i. p. 244). Fruticosa, ramosa, glabra; foliis linearibus, oblongis, glabris, coriaceis; racemis terminalibus; floribus pedunculatis; sepalis 4, cruciatis, duobus majoribus exteriori- bus ovatis acutis, interioribus ovatis; petalis 4, lanceolatis, unguicu- latis, minutis; staminibus 4; toro elongato; ovario stipitato, glandu- loso; capsula baccata; seminibus teretibus, glandulosis.—*Stræmia longifolia*, R. Br. in Append. Salt. Abyss. n. 64.

Hab. Aden (*Hook. fil.*! *T. Anders.*).

Distr. In Abyssinia!

Frutex ramosus, glaber, foliis petiolis pedunculis sepalis ramisque junio- ribus minutissime pruinosis. *Folia* 1½–2 unc. longa. *Torus* elongatus, 8 lin. longus, stipitem æquans. *Flores* violacei?

In the Hookerian Herbarium there is a glabrous specimen of *Cadaba Indica*, Lam., which, except by its having the pale-yellow flowers of that species, I cannot distinguish from some broad-leaved herbaceous specimens of *C. longifolia* from Aden. The normal states of *C. longifolia* and *C. Indica* are, however, markedly different.

3. CAPPARIS, *Linn.*

1. C. GALEATA (*Fresen. in Mus. Senck.* ii. p. 111). Fruticosa, glauca, ramis diffusis, foliosis; foliis petiolatis, ovatis, crassis, mucrone recurvo uncinatis; stipulis duabus, spinosis; floribus solitariis, axillaribus; pedunculo foliis longiore, erecto, in fructu deflexo; sepalis 4, sepalo maximo galeato; petalis subrotundis, glabris; staminibus numerosis; fructu baccato, pyriformi, angulato; thecaphoro longo, pedunculum æquante; seminibus reniformibus, testa crustacea.—*C. Murrayana*, Grah. Cat., et Wight, Icones, t. 379. *C. cartilaginea*, Dcne. in Ann. Sc. Nat. ser. 2. vol. iii. p. 273. *C. uncinata*, Edgew. in Journ. Soc. Asiat. Bengal. xvi. p. 1213.

Hab. Aden, in rupibus (*Edgew., Hook. fil. et T.! T. Anders.*).

Distr. In Arabia Petræa! Ægypto! Scinde! in ora occidentali peninsulæ Indiæ orientalis.

Frutex glaucus, ramis junioribus pulverulentis, *stipulis* aurantiacis uncinatis. *Folia* cartilaginea, 1½–2 unc. longa, 1–2 unc. lata; petiolus foliis brevior. *Petala* et stamina alba, denique pallide purpurea aut purpureo-rubra. *Fructus* maturus ruber, 8–10-costatus, 4 unc. longus, 1½ unc. latus. *Stipes* 2 unc. longus.

It is impossible to distinguish this plant by any essential characters from states of that protean species *Capparis spinosa*, L.

To *Capparis spinosa* I unite *C. Ægyptiaca*, Lam., *C. herbacea*, Willd., *C. ovata*, Bieber, *C. rupestris*, Linn., *C. obovata*, Royle, *C. ovata*, Desf., *C. mucronifolia* and *C. parviflora*, Boiss., *C. Sicula*, Guss. In all of these so-called species, and especially in *C. herbacea* and *C. rupestris*, specimens are constantly occurring in which the slightly recurved mucro of the leaf, the large flowers with a more or less galeate sepal, large-angled fruit, and the glaucous state of the whole plant indicate an affinity to *C. galeata.* As, however, some of the steps are wanting, I have for the present kept *C. galeata* distinct from *C. spinosa*.

4. MÆRUA, *Forsk.*

1. M. THOMSONI (*T. Anders.*). Virgata, glaberrima; foliis linearibus, oblongis, coriaceis, mucronatis, brevi-petiolatis; floribus solitariis, pedunculatis; calyce tubuloso, brevissime 4-partito; fructu carnoso, stipitato, glabro, toruloso.

Hab. Aden (*Hook. fil. et T.!*).

Frutex glaberrimus, virgatus, foliosus, ramis paucissimis, cortice punctato. *Folia* in ramis floriferis fasciculata oblonga, in aliis alterna linearia. *Thecaphorus* pedunculo longior.

Ordo III. RESEDACEÆ.

1. Reseda, *Linn.*

1. R. amblyocarpa (*Fresen.*).   Subpruinosa; foliis integris, superioribus rarissime ternatim incisis, ovato-lanceolatis, basi attenuatis;
floribus spicatis; bracteis deciduis, longe subulatis; pedicellis calycem
æquantibus vel longioribus; sepalis 6, inæqualibus, linearibus, deciduis; petalis 5, duobus majoribus 5–10-partitis, tribus brevioribus bi-
partitis vel integris; capsulis obovatis, obtuse tridentatis; seminibus
minutis, reniformibus, nigris, asperulis.
Hab. Aden, juxta mare (*Edgew., Hook. fil. et T.! Madden! Schomburgk!*
Harvey! T. Anders.).
Distr. In Abyssinia!
Herba ramosa, subpruinosa.   *Caulis* perennis, striatus, angulosus. *Folia*
plerumque integra, utrinque acuta, in petiolum attenuata, 2 unc. longa,
3 lin.–½ unc. lata.   *Flores* parvi, bracteis deciduis.   *Capsula* triden-
tata, truncata.   *Semina* pauca, nigra, asperula, punctata.

After a careful examination of the species of *Reseda* in the Hookerian
Herbarium, and the study of Mueller's elaborate monograph of the order,
I can find no character, except the nature of the seeds, to separate this
species from *R. pruinosa*, Del., or *R. Aucheri* and *R. bracteata*, Boiss.,
which seem to be merely varieties of *R. pruinosa*.

Having made numerous dissections of all the species allied to *R. pruinosa*,
Del., I am convinced that no specific character of the slightest value can
be obtained from the number of the divisions or the shape of the petals.   I
consider *R. amblyocarpa*, Fresen., to be probably distinct from *R. pruinosa*,
Del., and its varieties,—from its having a perennial stock, almost always
entire leaves, a larger and denser spike, smaller flowers, and a slightly
different capsule containing much smaller, black and punctate seeds.
Reseda pruinosa is evidently an annual, with generally trifid leaves; it
has shorter spikes, larger flowers, and seeds nearly as large again as those
of *R. amblyocarpa*, of a dark olive colour, and with an almost perfectly
smooth testa.   Both, however, are pruinose.   The seeds of *R. pruinosa*
are also sometimes slightly punctate, and *R. Aucheri*, Boiss., which ranks
only as a variety of *R. pruinosa*, has often leaves as entire as those of
R. amblyocarpa.   In *Resedaceæ* the duration of the stock is probably an
uncertain character, subject to the influence of climate, and especially to
the amount of moisture.

Ordo IV. POLYGALACEÆ.

1. Polygala, *Linn.*

1. P. triflora (*Linn. Fl. Zel.* p. 269).   Caule erecto, pubescente pilis
adpressis; foliis subsessilibus, ovato-oblongis, apice rotundatis, utrinque
incano-tomentosis; floribus breviter racemosis; racemis pedunculatis.

sessilibus, 4–6-floris; alis obovatis obtusis, pubescentibus, capsula paulo longioribus; carina cristata, rosea; capsulis oblongis, marginatis vel emarginatis, ciliatis; seminibus pilosis.—*P. paniculata*, Forsk. Fl. Arab. n. 429. *P. obtusata*, DC. Prod. i. p. 326. *P. erioptera*, DC. *l. c. P. Vahliana*, DC. *l. c. P. arvensis*, Willd. sp. 3. p. 876. *P. Rothiana*, W. et A. Prod. Fl. Pen. Ind. Or. p. 37. *P. glaucoides*, Wight in Wall. Cat., sed non Linn. *P. grandiflora*, Wall. Cat. *P. serpyllifolia*, Poir. Wall. Cat. *P. Noucherensis*, Camb. in Voy. Jacq. iv. p. 24. *P. Arabica*, Edgew. in Journ. Soc. Asiat. Bengal. xvi. p. 1213.

Hab. Aden, in arenosis depressis (*Edgew.! Hook. fil.! Madden! T. Anders.*).

Distr. In Arabia Felici! Muscat! India orientali! Ægypto superiore! Abyssinia! Africa centrali! Senegal! insulis Capitis Viridis!

Ordo V. CARYOPHYLLACEÆ.

1. MOLLUGO, *Ser.*

1. M. CERVIANA (*Ser. MSS.; DC. Prod.* i. p. 392). Glabra, caulibus adscendentibus, teretibus, verticillatis; foliis glaucis, in verticillis irregularibus confertis, radicalibus oblongis obtusis, caulinibus linearibus; floribus 2–3, umbellatis; pedunculis elongatis, gracilibus; petalis nullis; staminibus quinque, seminibus glabris.—*Pharnaceum Cerviana*, Linn. Spec., ed. 1, p. 272.

Hab. Aden, in umbris arbuscularum atque in arenosis (*Hook. fil.! T. Anders.*).

Distr. In pen. Indiæ orientalis! Punjab! Ceylania! Siberia australi! Abyssinia! Senegal! Europa australi! capite Bonæ Spei!

Herba tenera, glauca. *Caules* teretes, 1–4-unciales; verticilla caulina foliorum 2–3-foliata.

2. SPHÆROCOMA, *T. Anders.*

1. S. HOOKERI (*T. Anders. in Journ. Proc. Linn. Soc.* v. p. 15). Caule erecto, lignoso, ramoso, cortice glauco; foliis in nodis oppositis, caulinis fasciculatis, carnosis, teretibus, apice obtusis, basi attenuatis; glomerulis pedunculatis, ebracteatis; floribus dense aggregatis; sepalis ovatis, concavis, mucronatis, florum sterilium linearibus, in fructu setaceis, setis integris; capsula, calyce et corolla squamis persistentibus inclusis.

Hab. Aden (*Hook. fil.*).

Fruticulus 2-pedalis, ramosus, glaberrimus, glaucus; caulis nodis oppositis foliosis. *Folia* 6-10 lin. longa. *Glomeruli* fusci, 1–3 lin. longi. *Pedunculi* erecti, 1–1½ lin. longi, bracteis 1–2, sepaloideis. *Utriculus* parvus, subchartaceus.

Ordo VI. MALVACEÆ.

1. HIBISCUS, *Linn.*

Sect. *Bombicella.*

1. H. WELSHII (*T. Anders.*). Caule suffruticoso, glanduloso, punctato, foliis petiolatis, late ovatis, 3–5-lobatis, cordatis, margine dentato-serratis, glandulis nigris utrinque punctatis ; petiolis superne hirsutis ; pedunculis axillaribus, solitariis, unifloris, petiolum æquantibus, supra articulum incrassatis ; involucello 10-phyllo, segmentis subulatis parvis ; calyce 5-dentato, nigrescente, glandulis hirsutis obtecto ; carpellis lanceolatis, pilis sparsissimis puberulis, extus cortice glanduloso reticulato ; seminibus pilis fulvis, dense gossypinis.

Hab. Aden, rarissime (*Hook fil. et T.!* *T. Anders.*).

Suffrutex glandulosus. *Cortex* subglaucus. *Folia* glandulis asperis scabra, ½–1 unc. longa, ½–1½ unc. lata ; petiolus 1–2 unc. longus. *Corolla* ignota.

I have named this very distinct species after my friend Dr. Welsh of the Bombay Army, the Civil Surgeon of Aden. I am much indebted to him for his kindness in accompanying me during my herborizations, and in showing me many of the rarer plants of the settlement, and among them this species.

Tab. I. Fig. 1, portion of leaf; 2, flower-bud; 3, section of the same; 4, sepal; 5, anthers; 6, single anther, showing mode of dehiscence; 7, cross section of ovary; 8, outer surface of a single carpel; 9, seed; 10, section of same; 11, embryo. With the exception of fig. 9, all are magnified.

2. H. MICRANTHUS (*Linn. fil. Suppl.* p. 308). Suffruticosus, caule pilis stellatis aspero ; foliis petiolatis, ovatis, subrotundis, indivisis, acute serratis, scabris ; pedicellis axillaribus, foliis longioribus ; involucello 5–7-phyllo, setaceo ; calyce breviore ; corolla reflexa ; capsula subglobosa ; seminibus sericeis.—*H. rigidus,* Linn. fil. Suppl. p. 310. *H. ovalifolius,* Vahl, Symb. i. p. 50. *Urena ovalifolia,* Forsk. Descr. p. 124. *H. clandestinus,* Cav. Ic. i. p. 1, t. 2. *H. micranthus,* Cav. Diss. iii. p. 155, t. 66. f. 1. *H. intermedius,* Hochst. in Schimp. Pl. Abyss. n. 2211. *H. parvifolius,* Hochst. in *l. c.* n. 2275.

Hab. Aden, prope sepulchretum veterum (*T. Anders.*).

Distr. In Arabia Petræa ! Muscat ! India ! Ceylania ! Abyssinia ! Mozambique ! Senegambia !

2. ABUTILON, *Tourn.*

1. A. DENTICULATUM (*Planch. in Herb. Hook.*). Caule tomentoso; foliis ovatis, cordatis, acutis, denticulatis, glauco-tomentosis, petiolatis ; pedicellis petiolo longioribus ; calycis segmentis acutis ; carpellis

8-10, truncatis, muticis, tomentosis, trispermis.—*Sida denticulata*,
Fresen. Mus. Sencken. i. p. 82.

Hab. Aden (*Hook. fil. et T. !*).

Distr. In Arabia Petræa! Scinde! Ægypto superiore! Senaar!

Ordo VII. STERCULIACEÆ.

1. STERCULIA, *Linn.*

1. S. ARABICA (*T. Anders.*). Glabra, cortice cinereo; foliis petiolatis,
rotundatis, late ovatis obtusis, vel subrhomboideis acutis, basi interdum subcordatis, integris vel crenatis, utrinque glaberrimis, stipulis
subulatis; racemis in ultimis ramis vel axillaribus, simplicibus, paucifloris, folio multo brevioribus; pedunculis glabris; pedicellis apice
pilosulis; bracteis minutis, subulatis; calyce ad medium 5-fido,
utrinque piloso, laciniis patentibus; floribus masculinis tubo stamineo
exserto, 10-lobato, glabro; folliculis 4, anguste ovatis, acutis, pubescentibus.—*S. Abyssinica*, R. Br. partim in Append. Salt. Abyss. et in
Pl. Javan. Rar. p. 227.

Hab. Aden (*Hook. fil. et T. !*).

Arbuscula 8-10-pedalis, glaberrima, foliata; *ramuli* abbreviati, paulo
incrassati; *ramuli floriferi* in nodis foliosis abbreviatis aut in longitu-
dine petiolum æquantibus, stipulis deciduis obtecti. *Folia* 3-5-nervia,
1-1½ unc. longa, 1-2½ unc. lata; *nervi* viridescentes; petiolus teres,
glaber, ¼-¾ unc. longus. *Racemi* ½-1 unc. longi, graciles. *Flores*
parvi. *Folliculi* teretes, subrostrati, fulvo-pubescentes, ¾ unc. longi, ½
unc. lati.

Tab. II. A. *Sterculia Arabica* (T. Anders.): fig. 1, male flower; 2, same
laid open; 3, anthers; 4, fruit, natural size. (Figures 1, 2, and 3 are
magnified.) B. Leaf and fruit of *S. Abyssinica*, R. Br., natural size.

I have examined, on two distinct occasions, the original specimens of *S.
Abyssinica*, R. Br., in Salt's Abyssinian plants in the British Museum, and
at the same time compared them with ten or twelve specimens of the Aden
species *S. Arabica*. I find that among Salt's specimens of *S. Abyssinica*
there is a fragment of *S. Arabica*, consisting of a portion of a branch with
three leaves, and a fruit of four follicles on a very short axillary peduncle;
and from this the description in the 'Plantæ Javanicæ Rariores,' of the fruit
and partly of the leaves, of *S. Abyssinica* was deduced. Though Salt's specimens of these two species of *Sterculia* are said to be from Abyssinia, they
are possibly from quite distinct localities; for that traveller, after touching
at several points on the east coast of Africa, visited Aden and Arabia Felix.
Whenever a favourable opportunity occurred, he seems to have collected
plants, but (judging from his herbarium in the British Museum) without
appending any notes or records of stations to his specimens. It is probable
that the specimens of *S. Abyssinica* were obtained at Mozambique, where

Salt spent several days ; and the fragment of *S. Arabica* mixed with the former species is most likely from Aden.

Had R. Brown seen flowering specimens of *S. Arabica*, he would doubtless at once have distinguished the two species, and, moreover, would have united his *S. Abyssinica* with his other species *S. Triphaca*, described from an imperfect specimen in fruit in the Paris Herbarium, collected by Loureiro at Mozambique, and which seems to have been considered distinct by Brown, on account of the fruit differing from what he mistook for the fruit of *S. Abyssinica*, but which I have above shown to be the fruit of *S. Arabica*.

Figure B. of Plate II. is taken from a *Sterculia* in the Hookerian Herbarium, from near Mozambique, named *S. ipomeæfolia*, Gerke, a careful comparison of which with the original specimens of *S. Abyssinica*, R. Brown, convinces me that it is certainly the same as that species. *S. Arabica* is easily distinguished from *S. Abyssinica* by its short-petioled, rotund, rarely acute, and perfectly glabrous leaves, very short, axillary, simple, nearly glabrous racemes, and by the markedly different fruit, which is only half the size of that of *S. Abyssinica*.

The leaves, petioles, and peduncles of *S. Abyssinica*, besides possessing other and more important characters, are always more or less tomentose.

Ordo VIII. TILIACEÆ.

1. Corchorus, *Linn.*

1. C. Antichorus (*Roemschal, Nomencl. Bot.*, ed. 3, p. 158). Caulibus prostratis diffusis ; foliis petiolatis, subrotundis, ellipticis, plicato-crenatis, serratis ; floribus axillaribus, binis ; capsulis siliquæformibus, lanceolatis, deflexis, quadrivalvis, glabris.—*Antichorus depressus*, Linn. Mant. p. 64. *Jussiæa edulis*, Forsk. Descr. p. 210. *Corchorus fruticulosus*, Vis. Pl. Ægypt. et Nubia, p. 21, t. 3. p. 2. *Corchorus humilis*, Munro in Hort. Agrensi. .

Hab. Aden (*Hook. fil. et T.*! *Madden*! *T. Anders.*).

Distr. In Arabia Felici! Muscat! Scinde! India boreali-occid.! atque ad Madras! Africa boreali! insulis Capitis Viridis.

2. Grewia, *Juss.*

1. G. populifolia (*Vahl, Symb.* i. p. 33). Caule fruticoso, virgato, ramulis pilis stellatis sparse vestitis ; foliis alternis, brevi-petiolatis, orbiculatis, dentato-crenatis, 3–5-venosis, glaberrimis, junioribus subtus pilis stellatis pubescentibus ; pedunculis solitariis pubescentibus, unifloris, rarissime bifloris, folio brevioribus, bracteolis duabus oppositis ; sepalis lineari-lanceolatis, extus pubescentibus, corolla longioribus ; petalis linearibus, breviter bifidis ; stylo staminibus longiore ; stigmate 4-lobato ; drupis 2–4-lobatis, pyrenis globosis glabris vel pilis sim-

plicibus puberulis.—*G. betulæfolia*, Roth. Nov. Spec. p. 249. *Chadra tenax*, Forsk. Fl. Arab. n. 338.

Hab. Aden, rarissime (*Hook fil. et T*!).

Distr. In Arabia Petræa! Persia! Scinde! India boreali-occid.! pen. Ind. orient! Senaar! Senegal!

Frutex plerumque glaber. *Cortex* pallidus, subnitidus, partibus puberulis, pilis stellatis sparse obtectis. *Folia* 1½-1 unc. longa, 4 lin.-1 unc. lata. *Pedunculus* 6-10 lin. longus. *Sepala* 6 lin. longa. *Drupæ* cortex flavus, nitidus.

Ordo IX. GERANIACEÆ.

1. ERODIUM, *L'Hérit.*

1. E. MALAPOIDES (*Willd. Sp.* iii. p. 640). Caulescens vel subacaule; foliis radicalibus ovatis, integris vel trilobatis, obtuse dentatis, basi cordatis, longe petiolatis, incano-tomentosis; pedunculis 2-3-floris; sepalis lanceolatis, acutis, 3-nerviis, dense pilosis; staminibus 5; stigmatibus 5; carpellis aristis barbatis.—*E. Arabicum*, Decaisne, Ann. Sc. Nat. ser. 2. vol. iii. p. 285. *E. bryoniæfolium*, Boiss. Diag. Pl. Orient. i. p. 61.

Hab. Aden, in arenosis maritimis (*Madden*!).

Distr. In Arabia Petræa! ad flumen Euphratem! in Persia! Beloochistan! Affghanistan! Punjab! Ægypto!

Herba perennis? depressa, incano-tomentosa. *Corolla* purpurea.

Ordo X. ZYGOPHYLLACEÆ.

1. FAGONIA, *Tourn.*

1. F. CRETICA (*Linn. Sp.* p. 386; var. subinermis, *T. Anders.*). Caulibus erectis, patulis vel divaricatis ramosis; foliis paucis, simplicibus, rarissime trifoliolatis, ellipticis vel linearibus, obtusis vel acutis, mucronulatis, carnosis, subsessilibus; stipulis variabilibus, plerumque parvis inconspicuis seu longis gracilibus, acute spinescentibus; pedunculo tenui, deflexo, unifloro; capsula acuminata, subglabra.—*F. Hispanica*, Linn. Sp. p. 386; *F. Arabica*, Linn. *l. c.*; *F. glutinosa*, Delil. Fl. Æg. p. 86, t. 28; *F. mollis*, Delil. *l. c.* p. 76, t. 27. f. 2; *F. latifolia*, Delil. *l. c.* p. 86, t. 28. f. 3; *F. cistoides*, Delil. in herb. Bové, n. 169; *F. Mysorensis*, Roth, N. Sp. p. 215; *F. Oliveri*, DC. Prod. i. p. 704; *F. Persica* DC. *l. c.*; *F. Bruguieri*, DC. *l. c.*; *F. acerosa*, Boiss. Diag. Pl. Or. viii. p. 124; *F. Aucheri*, Boiss. *l. c.* i. p. 62; *F. echinella*, Boiss. *l. c.* viii. p. 123; *F. grandiflora*, Boiss. *l. c.* p. 121; *F. Kahirana*, Boiss. *l. c.* p. 122; *F. myriacantha*, Boiss. *l. c.* p. 123; *F. parviflora*, Boiss. *l. c.* p. 124; *F. Sinaica*, Boiss. *l. c.* i. p. 61; *F. subinermis*, Boiss. *l. c.* p. 62; *F. Thebaica*, Boiss. *l. c.* viii. p. 121; *F. Californica*, Benth. Bot. Sulph. Voy. p. 10; *F. Chilensis*, Hook. et Arn. in Bot.

Misc. iii. p. 165; *F. virens,* Coss in Kralik. Pl. Alger.; *F. fruticans,* Coss, *l. c.; F. diversifolia,* Boiss. in Pl. Or. nov. ser. vol. ii. p. 113.

Hab. Aden, in locis arenosis convallium (*Edgew., Hook. fil. et T.! T. Anders.*).

Distr. In Europa Mediterraneana! Africa ab Algeria usque ad caput Bonæ Spei! Asia tropica et calidiore tota! Chili! California!

I have devoted several days on two occasions to the examination of a most extensive suite of authentic specimens of the many described species of this genus, and both times I arrived at the same conclusion—that there is but one species. The Kew Herbarium contains about 400 specimens of *Fagonia;* and these I attempted to divide into De Candolle's two sections, of leaves simple and leaves trifoliolate. The result of this first apportioning was, that the one-leaved section contained only ten specimens, while 390 remained in the section with trifoliolate leaves. The ten simple-leaved specimens belonged to the following species : 2 of *F. cretica,* Linn.; 1 of *F. Oliveri,* DC.; 2 of *F. myriacantha,* Boiss.; 1 of *F. parviflora,* Boiss., and 4 of *F. subinermis,* Boiss. The remaining 390 specimens, all of which were more or less trifoliolate, included all the described species of *Fagonia.* The next step was the selection from the 390 specimens of all the individuals in which trifoliolate leaves alone occurred. These amounted to 123 specimens, leaving 267 as intermediate with the simple-leaved and trifoliolate sections. These 123 specimens, in which every leaf was trifoliolate, comprised the following species entirely :—*F. latifolia,* Delil.; *F. mollis,* Delil.; *F. cistoides,* Delil.; *F. glutinosa,* Delil.; *F. Kahriana,* Boiss.; *F. grandiflora;* Boiss.; *F. virens,* Coss; *F. Chilensis,* Hook. et Arn.; *F. Californica,* Benth., and in part *F. cretica,* Linn.; *F. Arabica,* Linn., and *F. Sinaica,* Boiss. Only one specimen, however, of *F. Arabica,* Linn., and a few of *F. cretica,* Linn., had wholly trifoliolate leaves. The remaining section, of 267 specimens having both simple and compound leaves, consisted almost entirely of *F. cretica,* Linn.; and of *F. Arabica,* Linn., with *F. Sinaica,* Boiss., and *F. parviflora,* Boiss., with the exception of one specimen of each, and included the whole of *F. Bruguieri,* DC., *F. Thebaica,* Boiss., and *F. echinella,* Boiss., *F. diversifolia,* Boiss., *F. fruticans,* Coss, and *F. Mysorensis,* Roth. The form and size of the leaves and stipules are also most variable; in some specimens the leaves are nearly absent, and their place is supplied by the long and hard spiny stipules; in others, such as *F. subinermis,* Boiss., and in the plant from Aden, the leaves are for the most part simple with inconspicuous stipules, but in some states of this variety, as well as the other so-called species, the leaves are nearly elliptical, and the spines exceed the leaves in length. The shape and relation of the parts of the flower and fruit vary but little, though in a few cases there is some variation, of the extremes of which, Boissier has constituted two species under the names *F. grandiflora* and *F. parviflora.* There is also great difference in the amount of general pubescence; it varies from nearly perfect smoothness to viscosity, as in the states *F. glutinosa,* Delil., and *F. mollis,* Delil., and some specimens of *F. latifolia,* Delil. The species from North and South America, described as *F. Chilensis* and *F. Califor-nica*, do not differ in any respect from many states of *F. cretica*, to which I unite them. In *F. Californica* the spiny stipules are very short, and the sepals somewhat more lanceolate and a little longer than in the mass of specimens of *F. cretica*; but there is in the Hookerian Herbarium a spe-cimen from Arabia Petræa which it is quite impossible to distinguish from the Californian specimens. Dr. Hooker has also been unable to find per-manent characters by which to distinguish any of the described species from *F. cretica*, and he agrees with me in considering all as varieties of one variable species.

2. ZYGOPHYLLUM, *Linn.*

1. Z. SIMPLEX (*Linn. Mant.* p. 68). Caule prostrato, dichotomo, dif-fuso; foliis sessilibus, simplicibus, cylindricis, carnosis, obtusis; floribus parvis, solitariis, pedunculis brevissimis, in fructu deflexis; sepalis obovatis, apice cucullatis; petalis spathulatis, patentibus; capsulis ob-longis, subrotundis, 5-angulis, rugosis, loculis 2–5-spermis.—*Z. por-tulacoides*, Forsk. Descr. p. 88.
Hab. Aden, ubique in arenosis (*Edgew., Hook. fil. et T.! Madden! T. Anders.*).
Distr. In Arabia Petræa! et Felici! Scinde! Ægypto! Africa occid.! insulis Capitis Viridis!
Subherbaceum, perenne? viride, carnosum. *Caulis* rubescens. *Flores* parvi, numerosi, flavi.

Subclassis II. Calycifloræ.

Ordo XI. RHAMNEÆ.

1. ZIZYPHUS, *Tourn.*

1. Z. LOTUS (*Lam. Dict.* iii. p. 318). Ramulis spinosis, gracilibus; foliis ovatis, trinerviis, obsolete crenatis, subtus molliter tomentellis, aculeis binis, breviore recurvo, altero recto, petiolo longiore; floribus geminis, axillaribus; pedunculo petiolo multo breviore, deflexo; stylis duobus; ovariis bilocularibus; drupis subglobosis.
Hab. Aden (*Hook. fil. et T.!*)
Distr. In Arabia Petræa! Affghanistan! Algeria! Hispania!
Arbuscula. Cortex albidus. *Folia* 6 lin.–1½ unc. longa, 4 lin.–1 in. lata; petiolus 6 lin. longus. *Flores* inconspicui. *Drupa* solitaria, magnitudinis cerasi.

Ordo XII. TEREBINTHACEÆ.

1. BALSAMODENDRON, *Kunth.*

1. B. OPABALSAMUM (*Kunth, Gen. Terebinth.* p. 16; var. glabra, Hook. fil. in Herb. Hook.). Glabrum, foliis bi- trijugis, rarissime simplicibus,

integris; foliolis lateralibus ovatis, terminali obovato; calyce persis-
tente, campanulato, 4-dentato; petalis obovatis; staminibus 8, æqui-
longis; stylo antheris breviore; stigmate tetragono, obtuso. Fructu
, ovato, acuto, glabro, in sicco tetragono, biloculari, monospermo.
Amyris Opabalsamum, Forsk. Descr. p. 79. *B. pubescens*, Stocks in
Bombay Trans. 1847, et Journ. of Bot. i. p. 264.
Hab. Aden, in monte Jibeel Shumshum, ad alt. 1500 ped. (*Hook. fil.*!).
Distr. In Arabia Felici! Beloochistan!
Arbor mediocris, 15-pedalis, inermis, balsamifera. *Truncus* basi incrassatus. *Rami* divaricati, cortice cinereo, lævi, tenui. *Flores* monoici,
in apice ramulorum brevissimorum aggregati, subsessiles vel breviter
pedunculati. *Corolla* rubra. Lignum, cortex, fructusque odorem
balsamineum emittentes.

Dr. Stocks, in the 'Bombay Transactions' for 1847, says that this tree
produces a gum of no value, and that the resin of commerce is yielded by
Balsamodendron Mukul, Hook.

Ordo XIII. MORINGEÆ.

1. MORINGA, *Juss.*

1. M. APTERA (*Gärtn. Fruct.* ii. p. 315). Ramis divaricatis, nudis; foliis
ad raches reductis; rachibus bi- tripinnatis, 4–8-jugis, deflexis; foliolis
ovatis, obtusis, integris; paniculis erectis, axillaribus; floribus herbaceis, glaucis, pedicellatis; pedicellis bracteolatis, articulatis; calyce
5-partito, segmentis imbricatis, subæqualibus, oblongis; petalis ob-
longo-linearibus, reflexis; staminibus 10, inæqualibus; antheris unilocularibus; ovario libero, stipitato, 3-sulcato; fructu leguminiformi,
longe rostrato, ad apicem inter semina valde constricto; leguminibus obscure trigonis, 3-valvis, valvis extus longitudinaliter bisulcatis,
3-fastigiatis; seminibus turbinatis, trigonis, pendulis; testa crustacea.
M. Zeylanica, Linn. Sp. Plant. p. 546, et Delil. *Hyperanthera*, Forsk.
Desc. p. 67. *Balanus myrepsica*, Belon, Obs. p. 126.
Hab. Aden, spontanea in vallibus saxosis prope locum "Steamer
Point" dictum (*T. Anders.*).
Distr. In Arabia Petræa! Syria! Muscat! Ægypto superiore!
Arbor Arabica, 10–12-pedalis. *Cortex* cinereo-fuscus. *Ramuli* juniores
virides. *Raches* sæpissime foliola gerentes, pedales. *Corolla* pallide
flava. *Fructus* 8 unc.–1 ped. longus, deflexus. *Semina* oleaginea.

The seeds of this tree are said by Decaisne to yield the Ben oil of commerce; and he quotes the old traveller Belon as his authority. Guibourt
also says that the true Ben oil is derived from *M. aptera*, Gärtn.; and
De Candolle, who, however, doubts the distinctness of the species from *M.
pterygosperma*, is of the same opinion. Lindley and Simmonds, and more
recently Major Drury in India, agree in considering *M. pterygosperma*
as the source from which the oil is obtained. Guibourt also mentions

an oil procured from this species. In the Museum of Economic Botany at Kew, there are specimens of an oil from the West Indies, Honduras, and also from Madras, extracted from the seeds of *M. pterygosperma*, and in every respect identical with the true Ben oil. In India the natives use this bland inodorous oil for retaining the perfume of delicate flowers, such as jasmine. It seems that both species therefore yield an oil similar in every respect, but that Ben oil was originally obtained from *M. aptera*. This is the more probable from " Ben, " or " Ban, " the Arabic name for the oil, being coextensive in use with the geographical distribution of the Aden species. In India the oil of *M. pterygosperma* is called "Soujhna," the word "Ben" being there unknown. Linnæus seems to have considered the two as varieties of one species, as in the 3rd edition of the ' Species Plantarum,' p. 546, under *M. Zeylanica*, he remarks, " Semina ex Asia tribus membranis longitudinaliter alata fuere ; ex Africa vero membranis caruere."

Ordo XIV. LEGUMINOSÆ.

Subordo PAPILIONACEÆ.

1. ARGYROLOBIUM, *Eck. et Zey.*

A. ARABICUM (*Jaub. et Spach, Ill. Pl. Or.* i. p.115). Ramis diffusis, gracilibus, teretibus, pilis adpressibus sericeo-pilosis ; foliis trifoliolatis ; foliolis plerumque linearibus, sæpe ovatis, margine revolutis ; floribus pedunculatis, petiolis brevioribus, bifloris ; calyce adpresse sericeo, segmentis lanceolatis, oblongis, acutis ; corollæ vexillo subrotundo, emarginato, alis cultriformibus, obtusis ; leguminibus linearibus, strigosis, undulatis, rostratis, stylo persistente acuminatis ; seminibus 6-10, lenticularibus.—*Cytisus Arabicus*, Dcne. Ann. Sc. Nat., ser. 2. vol. iv. p. 78.

Hab. Aden, rarissime (*Hook. fil. et T!*).

Distr. In insula Neymen in Mare Rubro!

Suffrutex diffusus, ramosus, sericeo-pilosus. *Foliola* 2-6 lin. longa, plerumque angusta, linearia ; petiolus 4-6 lin. longus. *Pedunculi* axillares, bracteolati. *Bracteolæ* parvæ, lanceolatæ. *Corolla* flava, glabra, calyce longior, 3 lin. longa. *Stamina* 10, monadelpha. *Stylus* filiformis, persistens, glaber. *Legumen* 1¼ unc. longum, 1 lin. latum, basi calyce persistente vestitum.

Judging from the description only, *A. Bottæ*, Jaub. et Spach, from Jeddah, is probably the same as this species.

2. INDIGOFERA, *Linn.*

1. ARABICA (*Jaub. et Spach, Ill. Pl. Or.* v. t. 479). Argentea, sericea, ramulis diffusis ; foliis 3-5-jugis vel trifoliolatis ; foliolis oblongis, obovatis, mucronulatis, oppositis, stipulis subulatis, minimis ; racemis axillaribus, multifloris, foliis brevioribus ; calycibus profunde 5-fidis, seg-

mentis subulatis, setaceis ; vexillo oblique obovato, breviter unguicu-
lato, dorso sericeo, intus glabro, carina oblonga, biunguiculata ; leguminibus planis, oblongis, cuspidato-acuminatis, valvis carinatis.
Hab. Aden, in saxosis (*Hook. fil.* !).
Distr. In Yemen, provincia Arabiæ Felicis! ad ' Wade Katte " in Arabia Petræa !
Suffruticulus decumbens, 2–5-pollicaris, omnino sericeus.   *Folia* petiolata ; petiolus 3 lin. longus. *Foliola* 1–2 lin. longa. *Racemi* breviter
pedunculati. *Flores* conferti, fructu deflexi. *Corolla* coccinea. *Capsula*-2–5-sperma. *Semina* lævia, nitida.

This plant is described by Jaub. and Spach as being sometimes one foot
long ; the specimens I have seen are all small and stunted, ranging from
two to five inches in length.

3. Pogonostigma, *Boiss.*

P. Arabicum (*Boiss. Diag. Pl. Or.* ii. p. 39).   Ramis adscendentibus ;
foliis petiolatis, stipulatis, plerumque bijugis, foliolis oppositis, lineari-
oblongis vel lanceolatis, mucronatis, supra molliter pubescentibus,
subtus sericeo-tomentosis, racemis elongatis ; calycis segmentis subulatis, acutis ; leguminibus suborbicularibus, acutis, stylo persistente longe
apiculatis, monospermis.—*Psoralea Arabica*, Hochst. in Schimp. Pl.
Arab. n. 775. *Catacline sericea*, Edgew. in Journ. Asiat. Soc. Bengal.
vol. xvi. p. 1214.
Hab. Aden (*Edgew., Madden* ! *Hook. fil. et T.* ! *T. Anders.*).
Suffrutex 1–2-pedalis, sericeo-tomentosus.   *Folia* ½–1½ unc. longa ;
foliola 2–6 lin. longa, terminale geminum, fere duplo longius. *Racemi*
subaphylli. *Flores* solitarii vel gemini ; pedicellus 1–2 lin. longus.
Calyx sericeus. *Corolla* calyce longior ; vexillum extus sericeo-hir-
sutum, purpureum. *Semen* olivaceum, 1½ lin. longum.

4. Tephrosia, *Pers.*

T. Apollinea (*DC. Prod.* ii. p. 254).   Suffruticosa, diffusa, amulis
suberectis ; foliis petiolatis, 3–4-jugis ; foliolis oblongo-lanceolatis,
cuneato-oblongis ; floribus racemosis vel 3–4 axillaribus, pedunculis
brevibus ; calyce campanulato, dentibus subulatis ; corolla calyce
longiore ; leguminibus patulis, linearibus, rostratis, planis, pubescentibus, 5–12-spermis.—*Galega Apollinea*, Delil. Fl. Æg. p. 144,
t. 53. f. 5.
Hab. Aden, in rupibus (*Hook. fil.* !).
Distr. In Arabia Felici et Petræa ! Scinde ! Abyssinia ! Ægypto superiore !
Suffrutex incano-tomentosus, stipulis subherbaceis, acute subulatis.
Folia 1–2 unc. longa ; foliola ½–1½ unc. longa, 1½–4 lin. lata, petiolo
longiora. *Corollæ* vexillum extus sericeum, purpureum. *Legumen*
1½–3 unc. longum, 2–3 lin. latum.

5. Taverniera, *DC.*

1. T. glauca (*Edgew. in Journ. Asiat. Soc. Bengal*, xvi. p. 1214). "Glaberrima; foliis unifoliatis, carnosis, glabris, glaucis, rhomboideo-ovatis, suborbiculatis, emucronatis; stipulis 2, parvis, scariosis, cuneatis, acutis; racemis 5-10-floris; bracteis pedicello brevioribus, acutis, margine membranaceis; staminibus apice geniculatis, alternis brevioribus, decimo recto, multo breviore, geniculum vix attingente; legumine 2-articulato, setis introrsum arcuatis hispido."

" Next to *T. lappacea*, DC. ii. p. 339. Differs in smoothness, and the setæ of the legume are scarcely hamose; the stamens are more geniculate than is allowed to the generic character as given by DC. The pods are concealed by the withered, scarious, persistent petals."

" *Vexilla* magna, concava, per anthesin reflexa, subcarinata, breviter emarginata et calloso-mucronulata. *Alæ* angustæ, falcatæ, ellipticæ, basi truncato-auriculatæ, ungue brevi tenui vexillo plus duplo breviore. *Carina* vexillo major, obtusa. *Stylus* longus, basi tortuoso-geniculatus, filiformis, stigmate punctiformi apicali." No one has seen a *Taverniera* at Aden, except Mr. Edgeworth; and I know nothing of his plant, except from the description which I have quoted. If not identical with *T. glabra*, Boiss. (Diag. ii. p. 90), it is probably closely allied to it.

6. Rhynchosia, *Lour.*

1. R. pulverulenta (*Stocks in Kew Journ. of Bot.* iv. p. 147). Molliter subincana; ramulis teretibus; foliis trifoliatis, petiolatis; foliolis super velutinis, subtus reticulato-venosis, lateralibus oblique subrotundis, obtusis, subsessilibus, terminalibus rhomboideis, petiolatis; floribus axillaribus, racemosis vel subsolitariis; racemis abbreviatis, 3-7-floris; bracteis pedicello paulo brevioribus; calycis segmentis subulatis, acutis, inferiore cæteris longiore; leguminibus deflexis, basi attenuatis, falcatis, tomentosis, dispermis; seminibus ovatis, lævibus.

Hab. Aden, in vallibus arenosis prope littus (*Hook. fil. et T.* ! *T. Anders.*). *Distr.* In Scinde!

Suffruticulus perennis. *Caulis*, in exemplis Arabicis, subprostratus seu volubilis. *Vexillum* extus subpubescens, flavum, 2 lin. longum. *Legumen* 6-8 lin. longum, 2 lin. latum, *Semina* fulva, punctis nigris notata. This species is nearly allied to *R. Memnonia*, DC., but differs from it in the inflorescence, the length of the teeth of the calyx, and the colour and markings of the seed. In *R. Memnonia* the pubescence is more silvery-white, the leaves are more distinctly veined, and the pods are darker-coloured and broader than in *R. pulverulenta*.

Subordo Cæsalpineæ.

7. Cassia, *Linn.*

1. C. pubescens (*R. Br. in Salt, Abyss. App.*). Caule adscendente, obscure striato; foliis 6-9-jugis; foliolis oppositis, ovatis vel ovato-

oblongis, apice obtusis, rotundatis, emucronatis seu mucronulatis;
petiolis eglandulosis; racemis axillaribus, multifloris, folio brevioribus;
floribus breviter pedicellatis, bracteatis; bracteis subulatis, caducis-
simis; ovariis pubescentibus; stylis glabris; leguminibus oblongis,
subreniformibus, utrinque rotundatis, falcatis, dense velutinis, 2–8-
spermis; seminibus cuneiformibus, obtuse bilobatis, caudatis.—*C.
Schimperi*, Steudel, Nomencl. Bot., ed. 2, i. p. 307; *C. pubescens* et
C. tomentosa, Ehrbg. et Hemp.; *C. cana*, Wender. Linnæa, xii. p. 19.
Hab. Aden, in locis saxosis et glareosis (*Hook. fil. et T.*! *T. Anders.*).
Distr. In Arabia Felici in regione " Tehama " dicta! Scinde!

2. C. OBOVATA (*Coll. Mon.* p. 92). Caule erecto, striato; foliis 3–7-
jugis, petiolis eglandulosis; foliolis oblique ovatis vel cuneato-
oblongis, apice rotundatis obtusisve, plus minus mucronatis, glaucis;
racemis axillaribus, plerisque folia superantibus, multifloris; floribus
breviter pedicellatis, pedicellis apice incrassatis; sepalis subæqualibus;
corolla calyce duplo majori; antheris longe linearibus; ovariis subglabris; stylis glabris; leguminibus subreniformibus, compressis, utrinque obtusis, ad medium tumido-cristatis, 6–9-spermis, valvis transversim venosis.—*C. Senna*, Lam. Ill. t. 332.
Hab. Aden (*Hook. fil. et T.*!).
Distr. In Arabia Felici! Scinde! Pen. Ind. orient.! Abyssinia! Ægypto!
Africa centrali! Senegambia! Jamaica! Texas!
Suffrutex, species præcedente robustior, glaucus, partibus novellis pru-
inoso-glandulosis. *Folia* 2–5 unc. longa; stipulæ lanceolatæ, acutæ,
demum reflexæ, persistentes; foliola ½–1 unc. longa, 3–5 lin. lata.
Sepala glabra, nigrescentia, 4 lin. longa. *Petala* ovato-oblonga, obtusa, lineis nigro-purpureis notata, 5 lin. longa. *Legumen* stylo revoluto persistente apiculatum, glaucum, pilis simplicibus sparsissime
obtectum, 1–1¼ unc. longum, 6–7 lin. latum.

Subordo MIMOSEÆ.

8. ACACIA, *Neck.*

Ser. *Gummiferæ*, Benth

§ *Summibracteatæ*, Benth.

1. A. EDGEWORTHII (*T. Anders.*). Caule glauco, ramulis novellis sæpe
puberulis; petiolis subtomentosis; spinis rectis, longis, albescen-
tibus vel puberulis; pinnis 4-jugis; foliolis 6–10-jugis, linearibus,
obtusis, minute pruinosis; pedunculis folio brevioribus; leguminibus
linearibus, falciformibus, crassis, tomentosis, obscure striatis, 14-sper-
mis.—*A. erioloba*, Edgew.? Journ. Asiat. Soc. Bengal, xvi. p. 1215,
non Benth.
Hab. Aden, frequenter (*Edgew.*, *Hook fil. et T.*! *T. Anders.*).

Arbuscula ab *A. Farnesiana* foliis leguminibusque differens. *Legumen* 5 unc. longum, 4 lin. latum.

§ *Medibracteatæ.*

2. A. EBURNEA (*Willd. Spec.* iv. 1081). "Ramulis foliisque ferrugineo-villosulis; spinis rectis, nonnullis longis, eburneis; pinnis 2–4-jugis, parvis, glandula petiolari majuscula; foliolis 6–8-jugis, minimis, linea-ribus, obtusis, hirtellis; pedunculis axillaribus, medio bracteatis; legu-mine stipitato, anguste lineari, falcato, subplano, glaberrimo."

Hab. Aden (*Hook. fil. et T.! T. Anders.*).

Distr. In Affghanistan! India orientali! Ceylania!

Folia spinis sæpius breviora; pinnæ vix 2 lin. longæ; foliola conferta, ¼ lin. longa. *Legumen* 2–3 poll. longum, circa 2 lin. latum, glauces-cens.

As all the specimens of this species from Aden are in leaf only, I have given Mr. Bentham's description in the 'London Journal of Botany,' vol. i. p. 501.

Ser. *Vulgares.*

§ *Dicanthæ.*

3. A. HAMULOSA (*Benth. in Lond. Journ. of Bot.* i. p. 509). Caule cinereo; ramulis rubescentibus; aculeis ternis, infrastipularibus rectis, infrapetiolari hamoso recurvo; petiolis aculeatis; pinnis 2–3-jugis, inferioribus suboppositis seu alternis; foliolis 3–6-jugis, oblique ob-longis, obtusis, glabris; pedunculis axillaribus, demum folio longiori-bus; spicis laxis; legumine ovato, lineari, utrinque rotundato, mucro-nulato, indehiscente; valvis membranaceis, planis, glabris.

Hab. Aden, in vallibus (*Hook. fil. et T.! T. Anders.*).

Distr. Jeddah in Arabia Felici!

Frutex 8-pedalis, divaricatus, aculeis acutis horridus. *Aculei* veteres nigrescentes. *Folia* 1–1½ unc. longa. *Pedunculi* leguminiferi, 2½ unc. longi. *Legumen* 3½ unc. longum, 1½ unc. latum.

Ordo XV. CUCURBITACEÆ.

1. CUCUMIS, *Linn.*

1. C. PROPHETARUM (*Linn.* spec. 1436). Prostratus, albido-pruino-sus, scaber; caulibus tetragonis, striatis, flagellatis; foliis plerisque 3–5 palmato-lobatis, rigidis, fragilibus; cirris simplicibus; floribus solitariis, axillaribus; peponibus ovoideis, muricatis.—*C. Arabicus*, Del. in Cat. Hort. Monsp.; *C. amarus*, Stocks in Herb. Hook.; *C. anguinus*, Forsk.? Descr. p. 168.

Hab. Aden, in locis arenosis (*Hook. fil. et T.! T. Anders.*).

Distr. In Arabia Petræa! Muscat! Scinde! Africa centrali! Ægypto!

Annuus? ramuli graciles, angulati, fragiles, albi, punctis scabris pruinosis reflexis. *Folia* polymorpha et magnitudine variabilia, ovata vel cordata, plerumque 3–5-lobata vel subintegra, subtus reticulato-venosa. *Peponis* pulpa amara.

2. CITRULLUS, *Neck.*

1. C. COLOCYNTHIS (*Arn. MSS. in Wight Icon.* t. 498). Caulibus longissime prostratis, angulatis, sulcatis, angulis tuberculis asperis scabris; cirris simplicibus, exaxillaribus; foliis multifido-dissectis, supra glabris, subtus tuberculis prominentibus hispidis, albidis; floribus femineis in ultimis flagellis, breviter pedunculatis, calyce hirsuto; peponibus globosis, glabris.—*Cucumis Colocynthis,* Linn.
Hab. Aden, secus littus (*T. Anders.*).
Distr. In Scinde! Punjab! Ceylania! Ægypto superiore! Algeria! Hispania! Senegambia! insulis Canariensibus! insulis Capitis Viridis!
Asper tuberculis hispidis; flagelli (ramuli) 1–4½ ped. longi, arenam adpressi. *Flores* conspicui, viridi-flavi. *Pepo* amarus.

Ordo XVI. PORTULACEÆ.

1. TRIANTHEMA, *Linn.*

1. T. CRYSTALLINA (*Vahl, Symb.* i. p. 32). Prostrata, diffusa, papulosa; caule fruticoso, tereti; foliis oppositis, spathulatis, ovalibus; floribus axillaribus, congestis; staminibus quinque; stylo uno; capsulis dispermis, operculo cyathiformi.—*T. triquetra,* Rottl.; *Papularia crystallina,* Forsk. Descr. p. 69.
Hab. Aden (*T. Anders.*).
Distr. In Arabia Felici! India orientali tota!

2. ORYGIA, *Forsk.*

1. O. DECUMBENS (*Forsk. Descr.* p. 103). Caule prostrato seu suberecto, tereti; foliis alternis, ovatis, acutis, petiolatis; petioli basi margine scariosa; racemis laxis, terminalibus, rarissime axillaribus; bracteis subulatis, scariosis, suboppositis; calyce 5-partito, persistente; petalis et staminibus plurimis; capsulis globosis, 5-valvis, polyspermis.—*Portulaca decumbens,* Vahl, Symb. i. p. 33. *Talinum decumbens,* Willd. Spec. ii. p. 864.
Hab. Aden, a littore ad altitudinem 1000 ped. in montem Jibeel Shumshum (*Edgew. Hook. fil.!*).
Distr. In Arabia Felici! Scinde! Pen. Ind. orient.!, Africa australi!
Fruticosa, decumbens. *Caulis* 3–10 unc. longus, glaber. *Folia* subfarinosa, 4 lin.–1 unc. longa, 2–6 lin. lata. *Sepala* acuta, marginibus scariosis. *Corolla* violacea.

Ordo XVII. UMBELLIFERÆ.

1. PTYCHOTIS, *Koch*.

1. P. ARABICA (*T. Anders.*). Puberula, caule erecto; foliis gracili-petiolatis, pinnatis vel bipinnatis; segmentis ternatis, profunde lobatis, lobis cuneatis, 3–4-fidis; radiis 5–8; involucris pentaphyllis, laciniis setaceis, subulatis, acutis; involucellis 3–5-phyllis; petalis minutis, squamæformibus, apice mucronatis, mucrone involuto; carpellis 5–7? costatis, costis glanduloso-hirsutis.

Hab. Aden, in cacumine montis Jibeel Shumshum (*Hook. fil.!*).

Herba pusilla, 2–4-uncialis. *Caulis* teres, pilis patentibus puberulus. *Folia* herbacea, subtomentosa seu glabra. *Flores* inconspicui, in siccis albi. *Fructus* maturus ignotus.

Ordo XVIII. RUBIACEÆ.

1. OLDENLANDIA, *Linn.*

1. O. SCHIMPERI (*T. Anders.*). Caule adscendente vel subdecumbente, scabro-glanduloso; ramulis virgatis, sparse foliatis; foliis linearibus, acutis, margine revolutis, mucronatis, obscure glandulosis; stipulis membranaceis, setis 3, subulatis; cymis terminalibus; calycis seg-mentis brevibus; corollæ tubo longissimo, gracili; capsulis subglo-bosis, truncatis. — *Kohautia Schimperi*, Hochst. et Steud. in Pl. Schimp. n. 879; *Hedyotis* sp.?, Edgew. Journ. Soc. Asiat. Bengal. xvi. p. 1216.

Hab. Aden, in arenosis (*Edgew., Madden! Hook. fil. et T.! T. An-ders.*).

Distr. In Arabia Petræa! in regione Tehama Arabiæ Felicis! Muscat!

Perennis, 1–1½-pedalis, glabra seu scabrido-glandulosa. *Folia* 6–9 lin. longa, ½–1 lin. lata; *corollæ* tubus 5–6 lin. longus; limbus 3–4 lin. latus. *Corolla* fulva.

I agree with Mr. Bentham in following Asa Gray in uniting *Kohautia* with *Oldenlandia*, a genus distinguished from *Hedyotis* by the dehiscence; which is loculicidal in *Oldenlandia*, and septicidal in *Hedyotis*.

Ordo XIX. COMPOSITÆ.

Subordo TUBULIFLORÆ.

1. VERNONIA, *Schreb.*

1. V. ATRIPLICIFOLIA (*Jaub. et Spach, Ill. Pl. or. t.* 359). Suffruti-cosa, ramosa, pilis adpressis incana; foliis petiolatis, carnosis, infimis spathulatis, integerrimis, superioribus ovatis vel sublinearibus, cuneatis, rhomboideis, dentatis, rarissime bidentatis, subsessilibus; involucris

5-6-seriali-imbricatis, squamis omnibus inæqualibus, exterioribus sub-
coriaceis, acutis, subpuberulis; acheniis abbreviatis, truncatis, hirsutis;
pappo biseriali, exteriore brevissimo, setis lanceolatis, interiore corollam æquante, setis albidis, aristatis.

Hab. Aden, a littore ad cacumen montis Jibeel Shumshum (*Edgew.
Hook fil. et T.! T. Anders.*).

Distr. In Arabia Felici.

Suffrutex perennis. *Caulis* lignosus, 6-unc.–1-pedalis. *Involucrum* paulo
variegatum, pallide violaceum. *Corolla* 1-2 lin. longa, violacea.

2. VARTHEMIA, *DC.*

1. V. ARABICA (*Boiss. Diag.* vi. p. 74). Suffruticosa, glanduloso-tomen-
tosa, ramulis apice corymbosis; foliis lanceolatis, basi attenuatis, apice
mucronulatis, integris, utrinque puberulis; pedunculis terminalibus,
cymosis; involucri squamis lanceolatis, acutis, adpressis, exterioribus
brevibus, subulatis; acheniis subhirsutis; pappo biseriali, setis ex-
ternis brevissimis, rigidis, internis 15-barbatis.

Hab. Aden, prope mare (*Hook. fil.*).

Distr. In Muscat!

Species distincta. *Suffrutex* perennis, 8-unc.–1-pedalis, foliosus. *Folia*
1-1½ unc. longa, 1-2 lin. lata. *Corolla* flava. *Setæ* exteriores acheniis
triplo breviores. *Achenium* ½ lin. longum.

De Candolle describes *Varthemia* as having the pappus uniserial; in five
species that I have examined, in addition to the original species *V. Persica,*
the pappus is in two rows, the outer consisting of short rigid setæ.

3. IPHIONA, *DC.*

1. I. SCABRA (*DC. in Ann. Sc. Nat.* sér. 2. ii. p. 263). Glandulosa,
scabra, caule ramosissimo folioso; foliis lineari-lanceolatis, subpungenti-
acutis, sæpissime integris, interdum dentatis; floribus corymbosis; involucris imbricatis, lineari-lanceolatis, membranaceis, glabris; acheniis
sericeo-hirsutissimis, striatis; pappo multiseriali; setis aristoideis,
barbatis.

Hab. Aden, frequentissime (*Madden! Hook. fil. et T.! T. Anders.*).

Distr. In Arabia Petræa! Muscat!

Species in forma foliorum variabilis. *Folia* in plerisque rigida, spines-
centia, in nonnullis herbacea.

4. HOCHSTETTERIA, *DC.*

1. H. SCHIMPERI (*DC. Coll. Mem.* ix. t. 6). Caule erecto, striato,
glabro, basi interdum gossypino-tomentoso; foliis ovatis, mucronatis,
basi in petiolum attenuatis, obscure serratis, margine scabris; floribus
1-2 in terminalibus ramorum; involucris præmultis, lanceolatis, argute
spinescentibus, apice serrato-barbatis, glabris, exterioribus denium re-

flexis; acheniis apice truncatis, basi attenuatis, hirsutissimis; pappo uniseriali, rigido.

Hab. Aden (*Hook. fil. et T.* !).

Distr. In Arabia Petræa ! Scinde !

Herba annua ? gossypino-tomentosa vel subglabra. *Caulis* striatus. *Folia* ½–1 unc. longa, 2–5 lin. lata; foliorum margo punctis asperis scabra. *Involucri* squamæ sub-3-costatæ. *Flores* aurantiaco-flavi.

Subordo LIGULIFLORÆ.

5. BRACHYRAMPHUS, *DC.*

1. B. LACTUCOIDES (*T. Anders.*). Glaber; caule adscendente, tereti, gracili; foliis radicalibus obovatis, runcinatis, obtusis, margine dentato-ciliatis; caulinibus amplexicaulibus, sagittatis, subtus glaucis; floribus paniculatis; paniculis laxis, multifloris, pedunculis gracilibus, filiformibus; bracteis minutis, scariosis; involucris imbricatis; squamis exterioribus parvis ovatis, margine scariosis, interioribus longe lineari-acuminatis; acheniis utrinque attenuatis, angulatis, tuberculatis, paulo adpressis; pappo pluriseriali, molliter piloso.—*Lactuca Massavensis*, C. H. Schultz in Schimp. Pl. Abyss. n. 1462.

Hab. Aden (*Hook. fil. et T.* !).

Distr. In Arabia Petræa? Beloochistan ! Abyssinia!

The shape of the achenia and the sessile white and downy pappus remove this plant from *Lactuca*, with which Schultes associates it. Though it much resembles some of the other species of *Brachyramphus*, it can at once be distinguished from them by its slender-pedunculated flowers and loose panicles.

Subclassis III. Corollifloræ.

Ordo XX. APOCYNEÆ.

1. ADENIUM, *Ræm. et Sch.*

1. A. OBESUM (*Ræm. et Sch. Systema*, ii. p. 411). Fruticosum, caudice ramisque crassis; foliis ad apicem ramorum confertis, ellipticis, ovatis vel spathulatis, subpetiolatis, obscure mucronatis, integris, crassiusculis, eveniis, glabris, subtus glaucis; pedicellis solitariis vel geminis, subaxillaribus terminalibusve, villosis; floribus folio longioribus; calycis segmentis lanceolatis, villosis; corolla extus puberula, intus pubescente; limbi lobis rotundatis, obtusis.—*Nerium obesum*, Forsk. Descr. p. 205; *Pachypodium obesum*, G. Don, Syst. Gard. iv. p. 80. *Cameraria obesa*, Spreng. Syst. i. p. 641. *Adenium Hongel*, Bot. Reg. xxxii. t. 54, non DC. Prod. viii. p. 412.

Hab. Aden, in rupibus (*Hook. fil. et T.* ! *T. Anders.*).

Distr. In Arabia Felici !

Frutex 1–3-pedalis, succo lacteo. *Caudex* globosus, crassus, carnosus, ambitu 1–2 ped. *Rami* teretes, crassi, aphylli, dichotomi. *Folia* et *flores* in apice ramorum. *Corolla* purpurea, 1½–2 unc. long.; limbus 1 unc. latus.

Ordo XXI. ASCLEPIADACEÆ.

1. STEINHEILIA, *Decaisne.*

1. S. RADIANS (*Dcne. in Ann. Sc. Nat.* sér. 2. ix. p.339) Incana, villosa, caule erecto; foliis subreuiformibus, acutis, serratis, pulcherrime variegatis, petiolatis; pedunculis axillaribus, solitariis, multifloris; floribus umbellatis, pedicellis brevibus; calycibus 5-partitis, segmentis lanceolatis, incano-hirsutis; corolla calyce duplo longiore, glabra, limbo 5-fido, lobis erectis, lanceolatis, acutis, contortis, tubo 5 foveis instructo; folliculo ovoideo, villoso.—*Asclepias radians*, Forsk. Descr. p. 49.

Hab. Aden, rarissime, in arenosis (*T. Anders.*).
Distr. In Arabia Felici!
Herba perennis, odore mellis. *Folia* lurido-viridia, subtus violacea, 1 unc. longa, 1½ unc. lata; petiolus ½ unc. longus. *Pedunculus* tomentosus, 1–2 unc. longus. *Corolla* 5 lin. longa, violacea. *Folliculus* abortu solitarius, carnosus.

2. GLOSSONEMA, *Decaisne.*

1. G. BOVEANUM (*Dcne. in Ann. Sc. Nat.* sér. 2. ix. p. 335). Incanum, "foliis lanceolatis vel ovato-lanceolatis, sinuato-dentatis, crispis, utrinque pubescenti-incanis; coronæ squamis apice emarginatis, medio subulatis; folliculis ovatis, attenuatis, spinis innocuis instructis."— *Gomphocarpus pauciflorus*, Hochst. et Steud. in Pl. Schimp. n. 920.

Hab. Aden (*Edgew.*).
Distr. In Arabia Felici!
Herba perennis, incana. *Folia* opposita, linearia, lanceolata. *Pedunculi* extra-axillares. *Pedicelli* basi bracteolis setaceis instructi.

I have not seen Edgeworth's specimen from Aden, and have therefore adopted Decaisne's description, from the ' Annales des Sciences Naturelles,' and De Candolle's ' Prodromus,' vol. viii. p. 554.

Ordo XXII. CONVOLVULACEÆ.

1. CONVOLVULUS, *Linn.*

1. C. GLOMERATUS (*Chois., DC. Prod.* ix. p. 401). Caulibus præmultis, prostratis, teretibus, gracilibus, pilis adpresssis pubescentibus; foliis hastato-lanceolatis, acutis, mucronulatis, petiolatis; glomerulis axillaribus; pedunculis folio duplo longioribus; bracteis folinceis, lanceolatis, villosis, calycem paulo superantibus; sepalis ovato-lanceolatis, fusco-villosis; corolla calyce longiore, glabra; capsulis globosis; semi-

nibus glabris, lævibus.—" *Convolvulus capitatus,* Vahl " in Schimp. Pl. n. 731 et 784, sed non *C. capitatus,* Vahl.

Hab. Aden (*Edgew., Hook. fil. et T.* !).

Distr. Arabia Felici ! Scinde ! Abyssinia !

2. C. SERICOPHYLLUS (*T. Anders.*). Caule suberecto ? ramulis strictis, sericeis, elongatis ; foliis lanceolatis, acutis, basi in petiolum attenuatis, utrinque incano-sericeis ; floribus axillaribus, breviter pedunculatis, solitariis, geminis ternisve ; bracteis parvis, subulatis ; sepalis ovatis, sericeo-pubescentibus, submembranaceis ; corolla calyce duplo longiore, extus sericeo-hirsuta ; capsula globosa, glabra.

Hab. Aden (*Hook. fil. et T.* !).

Suffrutex perennis, omnino incano-sericeus, 2-pedalis. *Caulis* et *ramuli* teretes, virgati. *Folia* 3 lin.–1 unc. longa, ½–2 lin. lata. *Pedunculus* 2 lin. longus. *Calyx* 1 lin. longus. *Corolla* 3 lin. longa.

Species *C. microphyllo* (Sieb.) proxima, sed calyce et corolla parvis sepalisque obtusis facile distinguenda.

2. CRESSA, *Linn.*

1. CRESSA LATIFOLIA (*T. Anders.*). Incano-tomentosa, pilis adpressis, caulibus et ramis subtortuosis, foliaceis ; foliis ovatis, obtusis, integris, utrinque incano-tomentosis ; floribus ad apicem ramulorum, axillaribus, solitariis, sessilibus ; sepalis ovatis, acuminatis, tomentosis ; corolla calyce vix longiore, extus hirsuta ; staminibus inclusis ; stylis paulo exsertis, ovariis hirsutis ; capsula puberula ; seminibus glabris. —*Seddera latifolia,* Hochst. et Steud. n. 884. *Breweria evolvuloides,* Chois. Convs. Or. p. 112. *Seddera evolvuloides,* Wight, Icon. t. 1369.

Hab. Aden, ad altitudinem 800 ped. in montem Jibeel Shumshum (*Hook. fil.*).

Distr. In Arabia Felici ! Scinde ! Pen. Ind. orient. ! Abyssinia !

I can find no characters of sufficient importance to keep *Seddera* as a genus distinct from *Cressa.* The stamens, included in the dry specimens, are said not to be so in the living plant. Dr. Stocks, in a note on this species in the Hookerian herbarium, says that in the fresh plant the corolla is rolled back, so as to expose the stamens. Wight's figure (Icones, t. 1369) is merely a glabrous state of this species, which Choisy referred to *Breweria.*

Ordo XXIII. BORAGINEÆ.

1. HELIOTROPIUM, *Tourn.*

1. H. STRIGOSUM (*Willd. Sp.* i. p. 743). Fruticulosum, radice lignoso ; caulibus erectis vel prostratis, ramosissimis, omnibus pilis adpressis strigosis, canescentibus ; foliis ovatis-acutis vel linearibus, integris, margine revoluto, sessilibus ; racemis terminalibus, laxis, elongatis, dissitifloris ; floribus subsessilibus, solitariis ; calycis segmentis ovatis, rotundatis, strigoso-pubescentibus ; corolla extus pubescente, calyce

paulo longiore; nucibus rotundatis, hirsutis.—*Heliotropium brevifo-
lium* et *H. tenue*, Wall. *H. tenuifolium*, R. Br. Prod. 494. *H. fruticosum*, Forsk. *H. parvifolium*, Edgew. in Journ. Asiat. Soc. Beng.
xvi. p. 1216.

Hab. Aden, a littore usque ad cacumen montis Jibeel Shumshum
(*Edgew.*, *Hook. fil. et T.*! *T. Anders.*).

Distr. In regionibus tropicis orbis veteris, a Senegambia ad Siam, etiam-
que in regione tropica Australiæ.

Ordo XXIV. SOLANACEÆ.

1. LYCIUM, *Linn.* '

1. **L. EUROPÆUM** (*Linn. Syst.* ii. p. 28, *et T. Anders. in Annal. Nat.
Hist.*, ser. 2, xx. p. 126). Fruticosum, cortice albido vel purpureo;
ramis spinescentibus, spinis teretibus; foliis 2–5, ad basin spinarum
fasciculatis, obovato-oblongis vel oblongo-cuneatis; pedicellis e fasci-
culis foliorum interdum geminis, plerumque solitariis, unifloris, calyce
longioribus; calyce breviter 5-dentato, glabro vel puberulo; corolla
calyce duplo vel triplo longiore, anguste infundibuliformi, staminibus
inclusis.—*L. salicifolium*, Mill. Dict. n. 3. *L. indicum*, Wight, Icon.
t. 1403. *L. Mediterraneum*, Dun. in DC. Prod. xiii. p. 523. *L.
Edgeworthii*, Dun. *l. c.* p. 525. *L. orientale*, Miers, *Ill. S. Amer. Pl.*
p. 99. *L. Persicum*, Miers, *l. c.* p. 100.

Hab. Aden, secus littus (*Hook fil. et T.*! *T. Anders.*).

Distr. In regione Mediterranea Europæ et Africæ! insulis Canariensibus! Arabia Felici! Scinde! Punjab! Pen. Ind. orient.!

Folia punctulata, $\frac{1}{2}$–1 unc. longa. *Spinæ* axillares, nudæ, vel foliola $\frac{1}{4}$–
1 unc. longa. *Calyx* 5-dentatus, campanulatus, 1$\frac{1}{2}$ lin. longus, glaber,
punctatus. *Filamenta* inclusa, inæqualia, uno cæteris breviore. *Corolla* 4–6 lin. longa, cæruleo-purpurea. *Bacca* globosa, glabra.

Ordo XXV. SCROPHULARINEÆ.

1. ANARRHINUM, *Desf.*

1. **A. PEDICELLATUM** (*T. Anders.*). Glabrum, suffruticosum, ramis virgatis, foliis linearibus, plerumque integris, acutis, crassiusculis, inferioribus interdum bidentatis; racemis laxissimis, dissitifloris, virgatis;
pedunculis foliis longioribus, solitariis, unifloris; calycis segmentis
ovato-lanceolatis, acutis, glabris, margine subscarioso; corolla calyce
duplo longiori, ecalcarata, glabra; capsulis magnis, nutantibus; seminibus ovoideis, tuberculatis.

Hab. Aden (*Edgew.*? *Hook. fil. et T.*!).

Suffrutex glaber, 6-unc.–1$\frac{1}{2}$-pedalis. *Rami* graciles, virgati. *Folia*
integerrima, rarissime bidentata, linearia, glabra.—*A. pubescenti* (Fre-

sen.) accedit, sed ab eo differt glabritie, foliis omnibus linearibus, racemis dissitifloris, virgatis, pedicellis longioribus.

2. ANTICHARIS, *Endl.*

1. A. ARABICA (*Endl. Nov. Stirp. Decad.* p. 23). Erecta, glutinosa,
foliis alternis, ovato- vel lineari-oblongis, obtusis, petiolatis, pubescenti-
glutinosis; pedunculis axillaribus, unifloris, infra medium bibracteo-
latis; corolla tubulosa, fauce elongata, ampla; staminibus duobus,
inclusis; capsulis ovatis, acuminatis, rostratis, bisulcis; seminibus
numerosis, rugosis.—*Capraria Arabica,* Hochst. et Steud. Pl. Arab.
un. iter, n. 748. *Meissarrhena tomentosa,* R. Br. in Salt, Abyss. app.
Hab. Aden (*Edgew. Hook. fil.* !).
Distr. In Arabia Felici! Scinde!
Herba annua, glutinosa, pubescens. *Caulis* teres, erectus, 4–9-unc.
Folia 5 lin.-1 unc. longa, 1–3 lin. lata. *Pedunculus* 2–3 lin. longus.
Corolla 4-5 lin. longa, glabra, venosa, cærulea. *Capsula* puberula,
2½–3 lin. longa.

3. LINDENBERGIA, *Lehm.*

1. L. SINAICA (*Benth. Scroph. Ind.* p. 22). Villosa, ramis erectis, divaricatis; foliis subrotundato-ovatis, petiolatis, grosse crenato-den-
tatis, floralibus subsessilibus; racemis elongatis, terminalibus, foliaceis; floribus oppositis, secundis; calyce campanulato; corolla calyce
triplo longiore, labio superiore erecto, inferiore breviore; staminibus
4; capsula ovoidea, bisulca, pubescente.—*Bovea Sinaica,* Dcne. Ann.
Sc. sér. 2. ii. p. 253.
Hab. Aden, in puteis veteribus (*Hook. fil. et T.* ! *T. Anders.*).
Distr. In Arabia Petræa! et Felici!
Herba viscosa, villosa. *Caulis* perennis. *Folia* 4 lin.-1 unc. longa, 2–7
lin. lata. *Racemi* semipedales ad pedales; flores remoti vel rarissime
conferti. *Calyx* folia floralia superans. *Corolla* 5-7 lin. longa, flava.

4. CAMPYLANTHUS, *Roth.*

1 C. JUNCEUS (*Edgew. in Journ. Asiat. Soc. Bengal,* xvi. p. 1217). Glaber, ramis elongatis, virgatis, subaphyllis; foliis linearibus, acutis, integerrimis, crassiusculis, caulinibus parvis subulatis; racemis elongatis,
virgatis, terminalibus; floribus alternis, pedicellatis, secundis; pedicellis
brevibus, basi bibracteatis, unifloris; calyce 5-partito, segmentis lanceolatis acutis; corolla calyce multo longiore, tubo elongato incurvo,
limbo patente subæquali; staminibus duobus; antheris demum ad con-
fluentia loculorum unilocularibus; seminibus numerosis, orbicularibus,
compressis, marginatis.
Hab. Aden (*Edgew., Hook. fil. et T.* ! *Madden* ! *T. Anders.*).
Distr. In Scinde?
Suffrutex glaber, subglaucus, 1- 3-pedalis. *Folia* inferiora, 1–2½ unc.

longa, 1–2 lin. lata, breviter petiolata. *Racemi* 6, semipedales ad
pedales. *Pedicelli* 1–2 lin. longi. *Bracteæ* minute ciliatæ. Corollæ
tubus 3 lin. longus; limbus 3 lin. latus; lobi ovati. *Corolla* flavo-
albida.

Ordo XXVI. ACANTHACEÆ.

1. BLEPHARIS, *Juss.*

1. B. EDULIS (*Pers. Synops.* ii. p. 180). Subacaulis, ramis nullis vel
divaricatis, prostratis suberectisve, plerumque pubescenti-velutinis
vel hirsutis; foliis ovato-linearibus, grosse spinoso-dentatis; tuberculis piliferis, utrinque scabris; spicis columnaribus vel abbreviatis,
quadrifariis; bracteis ovato-lanceolatis, spinoso-acuminatis, 5–7-ner-
viis, margine dentatis, 5–7 spinis; bracteolis linearibus, lanceolatis;
calycis sepalis membranaceis, tomentosis, inferiore trinervi integra,
superiore binervi bidentata, lateralibus subulatis uninerviis; capsulis
glabris, dispermis; seminibus pilis adpressis, fusco-incanis.—*Acanthus
Delilii*, Sp. Syst. iii. p. 819. *Acanthus pectinatus*, Willd. n. 11727.
Acanthus edulis,Vahl, Symb. i. p.48, et Forsk. Descr. p. 114. *Acanthodium spicatum*, Del. Fl. Ægypt. p. 97, t. 33. f. 3. *Ruellia ciliaris*, Linn.
Mant. p. 89. *Ruellia Persica*, Burm. Pl. Ind. p. 135. *Acanthodium
sinuatum?* β. *nanum*, Nees, DC. Prod. xi. p. 274. *Acanthus im-
bricatus*, Edgew. in Journ. Asiat. Soc. Beng. xvi. p. 1217.
Hab. Aden, in convallibus glareosis (*Edgew., Hook. fil. et T.*! *Madden!
T. Anders.*).
Distr. In Arabia Petræa! littoribus Sinus Persici! Scinde! Ægypto su-
periore! Nubia!
Fruticulus perennis, horridus, subacaulis, sæpe spica sola constitutus.
Spicæ 2–6 unc. longæ. *Bracteæ* rigide pungentes, 1½ unc. longæ. *Co-
rolla* azureo-cærulea.

Ordo XXVII. VERBENACEÆ.

1. BOUCHEA, *Cham.*

1. B. MARRUBIIFOLIA (*Schauer in DC. Prod.* xii. p. 558). Dichotoma, velutina, ramis teretibus; foliis ovatis petiolatis, serrato-dentatis,
supra glabriusculis, subtus incano-velutinis, rugoso-reticulatis; spicis
terminalibus, multifloris; bracteis lanceolato-subulatis, parvis; floribus
alternis, sessilibus; calyce 5-angulato, plicato, 5-dentato; corolla calyce
duplo longiore, hypocraterimorpha; staminibus 4, inclusis; capsulis
calyce inclusis, dicoccis, coccis demum dissilicentibus.—*Chascanum
marrubiifolium*, Fenzl, in Kotschy, Pl. Nub. n. 32.
Hab. Aden, in locis depressis (*Hook. fil.*! *T. Anders.*).
Distr. In Scinde! Ægypto!

Ordo XXVIII. LABIATÆ.

1. Lavandula, *Linn.*

1. L. setifera (*T. Anders.*). Glabra, caulibus subaphyllis, subtetra-
gonis, fere 6-costato-striatis ; foliis pinnatis, segmentis linearibus, integris vel dentatis, crassiusculis ; bracteis (foliis floralibus) alternis, unifloris, membranaceis, basi dilatatis, longe setaceis, calyce duplo longioribus ; spicis terminalibus, simplicibus, densis ; calyce 15-nervio, 5-
dentato, velutino.

Hab. Aden (*Hook. fil. et T.*).

Subherbacea. Caules virgati, subnudi, glabri, semipedales. *Folia* pilis
sparsissimis glabriuscula. *Spicæ* 1-1½ unc. longæ, velutinæ. *Calyx*
2 lin. longus. Corollam non vidi.

Ordo XXIX. PLUMBAGINEÆ.

1. Statice, *Willd.*

1. S. axillaris (*Forsk. Descr.* p. 58). Fruticosa, glabra, caulibus
divaricatis, foliosis ; foliis oblongo- vel lanceolato-spathulatis, acutius-
culis, carnosis, glaucis, in petiolum attenuatis ; petiolo basi fusco,
caulem vaginante ; scapis axillaribus vel subterminalibus, paniculatis,
paulo angulatis ; floribus confertis ; spicis breviusculis, secundis, spiculis
2-3-floris ; bracteis persistentibus, coriaceis, fuscis, margine subalbido,
superiore involuta enervi obtusa, inferioribus triplo majore ; calyce
infundibuliformi, basi hispido, persistente, 5-costato, limbo hyalino,
lobis obtusis.—*S. Bovei,* Jaub. et Spach, Ill. Pl. Or. i. t. 86. *S. lanceolata,* Edgew. Journ. Asiat. Soc. Beng. xvi. p. 1218.

Hab. Aden. in littore, etiam in cacumine montis Jibeel Shumshum
(*Edgew., Hook. fil. et T. Madden, T. Anders.*).

Distr. In littoribus Arabicis Maris Rubri !

Species distincta sed *S. Arabicæ* et *S. Stocksii* affinis, ab eis differt forma
foliorum et petiolorum, paniculis, bracteis calycibusque.

Ordo XXX. SALVADORACEÆ.

1. Salvadora, *Linn.*

1. S. persica (*Linn. Spec. Plant.* vol. i. p. 122). Adscendens, cortice
glauco ; foliis oppositis, petiolatis, ovatis, lineari-lanceolatis, acutis,
mucronulatis, eveniis, subcarnosis, glaucis ; stipulis inconspicuis ; paniculis in ultimis ramorum, oppositis, folia superantibus, multifloris ;
floribus in ramulis paniculæ sessilibus ; calyce 4-partito, segmentis
ovatis, obtusis ; corolla calyce paulo longiore, membranacea, profunde
4-fida ; lobis ovatis, apice rotundatis, concavis ; staminibus quatuor,
corollæ lobis alternis ; stylo abbreviato, incrassato ; bacca globosa, gla-

bra, calyce corollaque persistentibus basi cincta.—*S. paniculata*, Zuc-
car. *S. crassinervia*, Hochst. in Schimp. Pl. Abyss. n. 2218.

Hab. Aden (*Edgew., Hook. fil. et T.! T. Anders.*).

Distr. In Arabia Petræa! Scinde! Abyssinia! Ægypto! Africa centrali!

Arbuscula divaricata, glauca, 2–6-pedalis. *Folia* coriacea, 1½–4 unc.
longa, 5 lin.–1 unc. lata; petiolus 2–4 lin. longus. *Bacca* matura
rubra! magnitudinis pisi parvi.

This plant is the original species on which Linnæus's genus was founded.
Roxburgh in his ' Coromandel Plants,' p. 26, tab. 26, referred the common
Indian species (*S. indica* of Wight's ' Icones') to *S. persica*, Linn., from
which, however, it is quite distinct.

Salvadora Persica, L., is found in India only in Scinde, and perhaps in
the Punjab. The *Salvadora Indica* and *Stocksii* of Wight (*L. Persica*,
Roxb., non Linn.) is distinguished from *L. Persica*, Linn., by its distinctly
pedicellated flowers, broader, always ovate leaves, and darker, scarcely glabrous appearance; it also grows to a much larger size. It is extensively
distributed over India and Ceylon.

A third species (*Salvadora oleoides*, Decaisne, in Jacquemont, Voy. Bo-
tanique, p. 139, tab. 144), found only in the plains of North-Western India
from Delhi to the Indus, is readily distinguished from the preceding species
by its virgate elongated racemes with very short spikelets, and always narrow-
linear-lanceolate, subsessile, thickly coriaceous leaves. This is evidently
the *S. indica*, of Royle's Ill. p. 319, of which, however, there is no detailed
description, and the *S. Persica* of Wight's ' Icones,' tab. 1621 A. It
forms a spreading subglaucous bush, from three to six feet high. It is the
" Puloo " of the inhabitants of the Punjab.

Subclassis IV. Monochlamydeæ.

Ordo XXXI. PHYTOLACCACEÆ.

1. LIMEUM, *Linn.*

Sect. *Limeastrum.*

1. L. INDICUM (*Stocks, MSS. in herb. Hook.*). Caulibus diffusis, sub-
prostratis, junioribus pubescentibus; foliis oppositis, petiolatis, ovalibus, rotundatis, acutis, mucronulatis, integris; petiolis basi scariosis,
vaginantibus; cymis simplicibus axillaribus, confertis, bracteatis, foliis
brevioribus, 4–10-floris; petalis unguiculatis, apice truncato-dentatis;
calycis segmentis ovatis, acutis, margine scariosis; staminibus 6–7,
petalis alternis; stylis binis; coccis duobus, glabris, monospermis.

Hab. Aden, in locis depressis prope mare (*Hook. fil.!*).

Distr. In Scinde! Nubia!

Herba glabra vel puberulo-viscidula. *Radix* perennis. *Caules* 4-un-
ciales-1-pedales, teretes. *Folia* 2–5 lin. longa, 1–3 lin. lata; petiolus
1–2 lin. longus.

Ordo XXXII. SALSOLACEÆ.

1. Traganum, *Delile.*

1. T. nudatum (*Delil. Fl. Ægypt. Ill.* p. 57). Suffruticosum, ramulis alternis, tortuosis, teretibus, albis; foliis alternis, oblongo-triquetris vel teretibus, brevibus, incrassatis, basi dilatatis, mucronatis, glabris, glaucis; floribus solitariis vel 2–3 confertis; Calyce 5-fido, segmentis lanceolatis obtusis mucronatis, basi pilis floccosis apteris; staminibus 5, exsertis; filamentis compressis, deflexis; antheris sagittatis; stylis duobus; utriculo depresso, calyce indurato occulto.

Hab. Aden, secus littus (*T. Anders.*).

Distr. In Arabia Petræa! Ægypto! Algeria! insulis Canariensibus!

Suffrutex salsoloides. *Rami* divaricati, arenam marinam adpressi. *Folia* crassa, carnosa, brevia, sæpe late subulata, subpungenti-mucronata, succo aqueo plena.

Ordo XXXIII. AMARANTACEÆ.

1. Ærva, *Forsk.*

1. Æ. javanica (*Juss. Anns. Mus.* xi. p. 131). Caule herbaceo, inferne suffruticoso, ramoso, erecto, tereti, albido-tomentoso; foliis alternis, subsessilibus vel petiolatis, ovatis, oblongo-lanceolatis vel obovatis, superne eveniis, subtus venosis, utrinque incano-tomentosis; paniculis terminalibus, aphyllis, adscendentibus, plerumque elongatis, interdum abbreviatis; spicis alternis, sessilibus, cylindricis, flexuosis, albo-lanatis; floribus densissime confertis; bracteis membranaceis, glabris, ovatis, acutis; sepalis 5, obovato-lanceolatis, obtusis, tenuibus, lanatis; floribus raro hermaphroditis vel staminiferis, plerumque pistilliferis; stigmatibus 2–3; utriculo subrotundo; calyce incluso, monospermo.—*Celosia lanata,* Linn. Spec. p. 298. *Iresine Javanica,* Burm. Fl. Ind. p. 212. *Illecebrum Javanicum,* Ait. Hort. Kew., ed. 1, i. p. 289. *Ærva tomentosa,* Forsk. Fl. Arabico-Yemen. n. 584, et Descr. p. 170. *Æ. Ægyptiaca,* Gmel. Syst. Nat. p. 1026. *Æ. incana,* Mart. in Nov. Acad. Nat. Cur. xii. p. 291. *Achyranthes alopecuroides,* Lam. Dict. i. p. 548. *A. Javanica,* Pers. Synops. i. p. 269. *A. incana,* Roxb. Fl. Ind., ed. 1832, i. p. 671.

Hab. Aden, locis depressis in convallibus, et in monte Jibeel Shumshum (*Hook. fil. et T.! Madden!*).

Distr. In toto orbe veteri calido ab insulis Capitis Viridis usque ad Javam.

Perennis, 1–2-ped., albido-tomentosa, tomento floccoso. *Folia* forma variabilia, 5 lin.–2 unc. longa, 2–8 lin. lata. *Petiolus* semiuncialis aut nullus. *Paniculæ* 3–8 unc. longæ, graciles vel congestæ. *Spicæ* conglomeratæ vel laxæ, 2 unc. longæ.

2. SALTIA, *R. Br.*

S. PAPPOSA (*Moq. in DC. Prod.* xiii. pars 2. p. 325). Suffruticosa, cinerea, caule erecto, subtereti, pauce ramoso, cortice cinereo; ramis patulis, cortice viridi, puberulis; foliis alternis, subsessilibus, infimis in petiolum brevissimum attenuatis, linearibus, acutis, mucronulatis, crassiusculis, enerviis, glabris, glaucis; spicis brevibus, angustis, in ramis terminalibus; floribus approximatis, 2–3-bracteatis; bracteis parvis, una persistente, carinatis, mucronatis, villosulis; sepalis 5, exterioribus duobus altera paulo superantibus, ovatis, concavis, acutis, 4-nerviis, villosis, interioribus 3-nerviis; staminibus 5; filamentis sub-ulatis, compressis, basi dilatatis atque in cupulam connatis; antheris bilocularibus, ovatis; stylo simplici, tereti, staminibus fere duplo longiore; stigmate capitato, globoso, integro; ovario ovoideo, glabro, uniovulato.—*Achyranthes papposa,* Forsk. MSS.

Hab. Aden, in solo arenoso (*Hook. fil.!* *T. Anders.*).

Distr. In Arabia Felici.

Some confusion has occurred in the synonomy of this plant. Moquin-Tandon, in De Candolle's 'Prodromus,' has cited Schimper's number 977 as referring to *Saltia papposa.* In the Hookerian Herbarium this number is attached to a species of Convolvulaceæ, *Seddera intermedia,* Hochst. et Steudel (*Cressa* mihi), and, as such, is also quoted by Choisy in the 9th volume of the 'Prodromus,' p. 440. Fearing some mistake in the ticket, I wrote to M. Spach; and he kindly examined Schimper's number 977 in the Paris Herbarium, the specimen seen both by Choisy and Moquin-Tandon. He assures me that it is a true *Seddera.* M. Spach, in addition, corrects an important error in the habitat of M. Botta's specimens of *Saltia papposa* as recorded by Moquin-Tandon. M. Botta did not obtain his specimens at Mount Sinai, but in Arabia Felix—according to his ticket, in "Yemen, environs de Hamara et de Haïs."

Tab. III. Fig. 1, young state of flower; 2, matured fruit and two sterile flowers; 3, single bristle from a sterile flower; 4, one of the five sepals, with stamens and ovary; 5, showing relative position of stamens and ovary; 6, mature fruit, with the persistent stamens at the base. All are magnified.

Ordo XXXIV. PARONYCHIACEÆ.

1. COMETES, *Burm.*

C. ABYSSINICA (*R. Br. in Wall. Pl. As. Rar.* i. p. 18). Caule erecto, ramoso; foliis oppositis, sæpe uncinato-verticillatis, linearibus, lan-ccolatis, breviter petiolatis; stipulis scariosis, minutis, subulato-acutis; pedunculis in ultimis ramulis, axillaribus, floribus 3–4; bracteis op-positis, pungentibus, reflexis, villosis, demum aristis pinnatis; caly-cibus 5-partitis; segmentis marginibus membranaceis, apice fim-briato-ciliatis, duobus exterioribus concavis, pungenti-apiculatis; corolla (vel stamina abortiva) 5-loba; petalis basi in urceolum connatis; staminibus 5, petalis alternis, basi corollæ adnatis; stylo filiformi, simplici; stigmatibus 3, ovariis unilocularibus, utriculo monospermo. —*C. apiculata*, Decaisne in Ann. Sc. Nat. sér. 2. ii. p. 244. *Ceratonychia nidus*, Edgew. in Jour. Asiat. Soc. Beng. xvi. p. 1215.

Hab. Aden (*Edgew., Hook. fil.!*).

Distr. In Arabia Petræa! Muscat! secus littus Sinus Persici! Scinde!

Ordo XXXV. NYCTAGINEÆ.

1. BOERHAAVIA, *Linn.*

† *Flores paniculati.*

1. B. ELEGANS (*Chois. DC. Prod.* xiii. part. 2. p. 453). Caule erecto, basi fruticoso, albido-puberulo; foliis ovatis lanceolatis vel linearibus acutis mucronatis, margine sinuatis, infimis petiolatis, superioribus sessilibus; paniculis terminalibus laxissimis, ramosis; pedicellis filiformibus, gracilibus; bracteis inconspicuis, oppositis, tomentosis, bracteolis duabus subpersistentibus; perigonio infundibuliformi, paulo inflato, limbo contracto plicato dentato; staminibus 3, inclusis; stylo uno, stigmate capitato-peltato; fructu ovato-clavato, tereti, obtuse 5 costatis, costis eglandulosis, sulcis pilis adpressis sparse puberulis.—*B. rubicunda*, Steud. Nom. p. 213.

Hab. Aden, ubique (*Edgew., Hook. fil. et T*!).

Distr. In Arabia Felici! Beloochistan! Scinde!

Suffrutex 1-3 ped., glaucus, puberulus. *Caulis* teres, obscure striatus. *Folia* superne viridia, puberula, subtus glaucescentia, rugosa, $\frac{1}{2}$-1$\frac{1}{4}$ unc. longa, 3 lin.–1$\frac{1}{4}$ unc. lata; petiolus $\frac{1}{4}$ unc. longus. *Perigonii* limbus glaber, 1$\frac{1}{4}$ lin. longus. *Fructus* pyriformis, 2 lin. longus; pericarpum in aqua mucilagineum.

†† *Flores umbellati.*

2. B. SCANDENS (*Linn., Sp. Pl.* ed. 3. p. 14). Suffruticosa, caule diffuse prostrato, elongato, glabro; foliis oppositis, petiolatis, rotundato-ovatis, acuminatis, cordatis, margine repandis, utrinque glabris; umbellis in ramis terminalibus; pedunculis axillaribus 3-7-floris; perigonio tubo subinflato, limbo late infundibuliformi; staminibus 3, exsertis, stylo brevioribus; stylo brevi, stigmate capitato; fructu clavato, truncato, ecostato, apice glanduloso, muricato, pilis strigosis hirtello.—*B. dichotoma*, Vahl, En. i. p. 290. *B. repanda*, Willd. Sp. i. p. 22. *B. scandens*, Forsk. Descr. p. 3. *Valeriana scandens*, Forsk. Descr. p. 12. *B. plumbaginea*, Cav. Ic. ii. p. 7. *B. Burchelli*, Chois. DC. Prod. xiii. part. 2. p. 455. *B. verticellata*, Poir. Dict. v. p. 56. *B. grandiflora*, Rich. Hohen. in Schimp. Pl. Abyss. n. 2309. *B. stellata*, Wight, Icon. t. 875.

Hab. Aden (*Hook. fil.! T. Anders.*).

Distr. In Asia tropica! Africa boreali usque ad Cap. Bon. Spei! Hispania! America tropicali, boreali, et australi! Australia! Insulis Galapagos!

This is an exceedingly variable plant; but even in its most aberrant forms the characters of the umbellate inflorescence, exserted stamens and style, and the elongated, clavate, ecostate, glandular fruit, can always be recognized.

Ordo XXXVI. EUPHORBIACEÆ.

1. EUPHORBIA, *Linn.*

Sect. *Anisophyllum.*

1. E. ÆGYPTIACA (*Boiss. in Cent. Euph.* p. 13). Caulibus prostratis, teretibus; foliis oppositis, inæqualibus, integerrimis, ovato- vel lineari-oblongis, obtusis, crassiusculis, pilis strigosis hirsutis; floribus axillaribus, solitariis vel 2–3, brevissime pedunculatis; involucro hirsuto, glandulis 5 glabris, dentibus 5, glandulis alternis, ciliatis, hirsutis; ovario stipitato, incano, hirsutissimo, stipite pubescente; stylis non coalitis; seminibus rubescentibus, demum albidis, transversim rugosis. —*E. Forskâlii,* Gay in Phyt. Canar. iii. p. 240. *E. arillata,* Edgew. in Journ. Asiat. Soc. Bengal. xvi. p. 1218.

Hab. Aden (*Edgew., Hook. fil.! T. Anders.*).

Distr. In Arabia Felici! India boreal.-occid.!

Herba pusilla. *Caules* strigosi, hirsuti, fragiles, 3–6 unc. longi. *Folia* pilis adpressis subincana, 2 lin. longa, ½–1 lin. lata. *Flores* et *capsulæ* minuti, hirsutissimi.

The plant from•Aden is so small and strigosely hirsute, with leaves not at all serrated, that it seems almost distinct enough to be ranked as a variety. Judging from his description, Edgeworth seems to have found the normal state of the species.

2. E. ARABICA (*Hochst. et Steud. in Pl. Schimp.* n. 756). Erecta, glaberrima; caule tereti ramoso; foliis oppositis, strictis, inæqualibus lineari-lanceolatis vel ovato-lanceolatis, mucronatis, glabris; stipulis angustissime lanceolatis; floribus axillaribus, plerisque solitariis; pedunculo glabro brevi; involucro pyriformi, glabro, dentibus ovatis, fimbriato-ciliatis, glandulis rotundis, intus basi ciliatis; ovario et stipite glabris; stylis divaricatis, ad basin liberis; stigmatibus bifidis; capsula angulata; seminibus lævibus, flavo-rubris.

Hab. Aden, prope mare (*Hook fil. et T.!*).

Distr. In Arabia Felici, in Tehama!

Suffrutex perennis, 4-uncialis, 1-pedalis. *Caulis* lignosus. *Folia* remota vel confertim approximata, 2 lin.–1 unc. longa, 1 lin. lata.

Sect. *Carnosæ et Arboreæ.*

† *Aphyllæ.*

3. E. SCHIMPERI (*Presl. Bemerk.*). Fruticosa; ramis erectis, teretibus, carnosis, trichotomis; foliis deciduis, 1–3, in ultimis ramulis, minutis,

ovatis, acutis, integris; pedunculis terminalibus, brevibus, teretibus, crassis, carnosis, 4-floris; floribus breviter pedicellatis, umbellatis, bibracteatis; bracteis ovatis acutis, basi truncatis, subherbaceis, integerrimis; involucris campanulatis; glandulis 5, concavis; dentibus obtusis, fimbriatis, glandulis brevioribus; staminibus 20, nonnullis exsertis; ovario stipitato, glabro; stylis infra medium coalitis; stigmatibus incrassatis, bifidis.

Hab. Aden (*Hook. fil.*! *T. Anders.*).

Distr. In Arabia Felici!

Frutex aphyllus, carnosus, pallide viridis. *Rami* patuli. *Folia* rarissime adsunt, 3–5 lin. longa, 2 lin. lata, herbacea, glabra. *Pedunculi* 4–5, in apice ramorum umbellato-conferti, 3 lin. longi. *Involucrum* viride; glandulæ et antheræ flavæ.

†† *Superne foliatæ v. foliosæ.*

4. E. CUNEATA (*Vahl, Symb.* ii. p. 53). Caule lignoso, cortice cinereoglabro, ramis rectangularibus, spinescentibus, pauce foliatis; foliis in tuberculis fasciculatis, cuneato-oblongis, cuneato-ovatis vel linearibus, apice obtusis vel obscure bilobatis, basi attenuatis, sessilibus, interdum petiolatis, utrinque tomentellis; pedunculis e tuberculis foliiferis, 3–4-bracteatis, 4-floris; floribus umbellatis, 1 centrali, sessili, 3 pedicellatis; pedicellis pedunculo æquantibus sed gracilioribus; involucro campanulato, tomentoso; dentibus 5, cuneiformibus, fimbriatis; glandulis 5, concavo-peltatis, glabris; staminibus numerosis; ovario stipitato, tomentoso; stylis ad medium connatis, apice subintegris.—*E. fruticosa*, Edgew. in Journ. Asiat. Soc. Beng. xvi. p. 1219.

Hab. Aden (*Edgew., Hook. fil.*! *Madden*! *T. Anders.*).

Distr. In Arabia Felici!

Arbuscula 6–10 pedalis, glabra. *Folia* et *flores* partesque juniores puberuli. *Folia* 2–8 lin. longa, 1–3 lin. lata. *Pedunculus* carnosus, teres, puberulus. *Involucrum* viride; glandulæ flavæ.

Descr. of Tab. IV. Fig. 1, leaf; 2, entire flower; 3, longitudinal section of same; 4, scale on petal of the male floret; 5, stamen. All the figures are magnified.

Sect. *Trithymalus.*

5. E. SYSTYLA (*Edgew. in Journ. Asiat. Soc. Beng.* xvi. p. 1218). Erecta, dichotoma; ramis angulosis, adscendentibus; foliis alternis, valde petiolatis, lanceolatis, lineari-lanceolatis, integris, mucronatis, puberulis; floribus axillaribus solitariis, sessilibus; involucro tubuloso, persistente, 4-dentato, dentibus fimbriatis, glandulis 4 concavis alternis; ovario pubescenti, stipite incrassato, tomentoso, stylis ad apicem coalitis, stigmatibus bifidis. Capsula erecta, subglobosa, puberula; coccis bisulcis, angulatis, angulis rotundatis; seminibus conicis, compressis, constrictis, testa crustacea, punctata, olivacea.

Hab. Aden, a littore usque ad altitudinem 1000 ped. in monte Jibeel Shumshum (*Edgew., Hook. fil. et T.*! *Madden*!).

Suffrutex 2-3-pedalis. *Caulis* dichotomus, striatus, subglaucus, plus
minus foliatus. *Folia* puberula, ½-1½ unc. longa, 1-3 lin. lata; petiolus 6 lin. longus.

Descr. of Tab. V. Fig. 1, entire flower; 2, longitudinal section of same;
3, petal and stamen of a male floret; 4, mature fruit; 5, ripe seed. All
the figures are more or less magnified.

2. Crozophora, *Neck.*

1. C. oblongifolia (*Ad. Juss., Spr. Syst.* iii. p. 850). Suffruticosa;
caule suberecto, floccoso, tomentoso; ramis dichotomis, foliosis; foliis
petiolatis, subpeltatis, oblongis, lanceolatis, acutis, dentatis, dense stel-
lato-floccosis, basi biglandulosis; racemis abbreviatis, in ramis terminalibus; floribus bracteatis, breviter pedicellatis, monoicis; floribus
masculinis calyce 5-partito stellato tomentoso, petalis 5 glabris, staminibus 8-10, filamentis subcoalitis; femineis calyce 10-partito, corolla
nulla, ovario sessili, capsula globosa tricocca stellato-glandulosa, seminibus rugosis.—*Croton oblongifolium*, Del. Ægyp. tab. 51. f. 1.
Hab. Aden (*Hook. fil. et T.!*).
Distr. In Arabia Felici et Petræa! Muscat! Scinde! Ægypto!

3. Jatropha, *Linn.*

1. J. spinosa (*Vahl, Symb.* i. p. 79). Fruticosa, erecta; ramis teretibus, incrassatis; cortice cinereo-glauco vel purpurascente; foliis alternis, petiolatis, rotundatis, 5-7-nerviis, 3-5-lobatis vel obscure 7-lobatis,
lobis oblongis, obtusis, obscure dentatis, utrinque glabris; stipulis
pungenter spinosis, subpersistentibus; corymbis pedunculis elongatis,
terminalibus, dichotomis, multifloris; bracteis parvis, basi dilatatis,
acutis, scariosis; floribus subsessilibus, monoicis; calyce 5-partito,
petalis 5; staminibus 8; ovario sessili; stylis convolutis, 3, liberis,
stigmatibus peltatis; capsulis rugosulis, lignosis, tricoccis, coccis
monospermis.—*Croton spinosum*, Forsk. Descr. p. 163.
Hab. Aden (*Hook. fil. et T.! T. Anders.*).
Distr. In Arabia Felici.
Arbuscula 7-8-pedalis, succo lacteo. *Caulis* aculeatus, rami incrassato-
carnosi. *Folia* 1½ unc. longa, 1½-2 unc. lata; petiolus 1-1¼ unc.
longus; stipulæ aculeatæ, nigræ vel glaucæ, 3 lin. longæ. *Corymbi*
4-5 unc. longi. *Flores* flavescentes, plurimi subsessiles, feminei pau-
cissimi, in dichotomia corymborum sessiles.
Descr. of Tab. VI. Fig. 1, entire male flower; 2, same laid open; 3, female
flower; 4, same with the floral envelopes removed.

Ordo XXXVII. URTICACEÆ.

1. Forskohlea, *Linn.*

1. F. tenacissima (*Linn. Mant.* p. 72). Suffruticosa; caule et ramis
aculeato-asperis; foliis petiolatis, orbicularibus, ovatis vel rhomboideis,

grosse serratis, utrinque scaberrimis, superne subviridibus, subtus
dense incano-tomentosis, nerviis subglabris, viridibus; capitulis axillaribus, sessilibus, geminis vel quaternis, 4-5-foliolatis, foliolis lanceolatis vel rotundatis, acutis, albidis, ciliatis, pilosis.—*Caidbeja adhærens*,
Forsk. Descr. p. 82.

Hab. Aden, rarissime, in locis depressis (*Hook. fil.* !).

Distr. In Arabia Felici! et Petræa! in oris Sinus Persici! India boreal.
occid!. Ægypto! Algeria! Hispania!

Herba 1-2-pedalis asperrima. *Caulis* lignosus, ramosus. *Folia* ½-1
unc. longa, ¼ unc. lata; petiolus 4 lin. longus. *Capitula* petiolum
æquantia; cilia involucri viridescentia.

Ordo XXXVIII. GNETACEÆ.

1. EPHEDRA, *Tourn.*

1. *E.* FOLIATA (*Boiss. in Kotsch. Pl. Pers. Aust. et Diag. Pl. Or.* vii.
p. 100). Fruticosa; caule striato, ramis angulatis, ramulis verti-
cellato-fasciculatis, teretibus, puberulis, junceis, elongatis, ramosis
remote articulatis; foliis quaternis, teretibus, subulatis, elongatis, mucronatis, basi membrana, caule vaginante connatis; spicis masculinis
lateralibus vel ad apicem ramulorum aggregatis, subsessilibus; staminibus 3; floribus femineis 3-9, in ramulis trichotomis terminalibus
pedicellatis, involucris margine scarioso-ciliato.—*E. ciliata*, Fisch. et
Mey. in Meyer, Monog. Gener. Ephedræ, p. 100.

Suffrutex 2-3-pedalis, gracilis. *Caulis* subglaucus, striatus; ramuli floriferi 2-4 unc. longi, subtetragoni, sulcato-striati, fasciculati. *Folia*
8-10 lin. longa, superiora sæpe bina. *Spiculæ* masculinæ 3-4 lin.
longæ, multifloræ.

Hab. Aden (*Hook. fil. et T.* !).

Distr. In Persia! Affghanistan! India boreal.-occid. !

Classis II. MONOCOTYLEDONES.

Ordo XXXIX. AMARYLLIDEÆ.

1. PANCRATIUM, *Linn.*

1. P. TORTUOSUM (*Herbt. in Herb. Hook.*). Bulbo ovato; foliis linearibus, attenuatis, acutis, viridibus, canaliculatis; scapo brevi, non sub-
terraneo; spatha breviter pedunculata vel subsessili, membranacea,
bifida, triflora; perigonii tubo gracili, limbo quadruplo longiore, limbi
laciniis linearibus, acutis, coronæ, ultra medium liberis, dentibus acute
triangularibus; stylo et filamentis coronam superantibus.—*P. tortifo-
lium*, Boiss. Diag. Pl. Orient. xiii. p. 18.

Hab. Aden, in convallibus saxosis (*T. Anders.*).

Distr. In Arabia Felici, prope urbem "Jeddah"!

Folia sæpe tortula, 6-10 unc. longa, 3 lin. lata. *Scapus* 2 unc. longus.

Spatha 2½ unc. longa. *Perigonium* album, tubo incluso 5–7 unc. longum.

My plant, though not in flower, is doubtless the same as Herbert's species. It grows in clumps in one or two of the narrow valleys in Aden. Boissier quotes Schimper's number as 676; but the plant in the Hookerian herbarium is marked 876. My description is drawn partly from my own specimens and partly from the MS. diagnosis of Herbert in the Hookerian herbarium.

Ordo XL. CYPERACEÆ.

1. CYPERUS, *Linn.*

1. C. CONGLOMERATUS (*Rottb. Gram.* t. 15. fig. 7). Glaucescens; radice fibroso, tomentoso, culmis erectis e denso foliorum cæspite plurimis, rare solitariis, striatis, obtuse triquetris; foliis erectis, rigidis, subteretibus, canaliculatis, mucronulatis, margine scabridis, basi culmis vaginantibus, purpurascentibus; involucro 3–4-phyllo, inæquali; foliolis 2, capitulum superantibus, uno inferiore, altero longiore; umbellis in apice culmorum capitatis, solitariis, subsessilibus, vel plurimis inæqualiter pedunculatis, radiatis; spiculis 5–20, sessilibus, oblongis, obtusis, compressis, imbricatis, multifloris; squamis ovatis, obtusis, pluriminerviis, carinatis; stylo trifido.

Hab. Aden, in locis depressis prope littus (*Hook. fil. et T.!* *T. Anders.*). *Distr.* In Arabia Felici! et Petræa! oris Sinus Persici! Ægypto! Algeria! *Planta* magnitudine variabilis, plerumque pedalis, sed marcescentia 2–3-uncialis; radicibus exceptis, glaberrima. *Folia* culmos non superantia; involucri foliolum foliis longius, 3–4 unc. longum, radii ½–1½ unc. longi.

Edgeworth does not enumerate this species among the plants found by him at Aden, but records *Cyperus effusus* and *Jeminicus*, Rottb., neither of which occurs in any of the Aden collections that I have examined.

Ordo XLI. GRAMINEÆ.

Tribus PANICEÆ.

1. TRICHOLÆNA, *Schrad.*

1. T. TENERIFFÆ (*Parlat. in Webb, Phyt. Can.* iii. 425). Caule basi plus minus repente, ramoso, pubescente, demum adscendente, foliato, nodis vaginisque tomentellis; ligula pubescente, ciliata; foliis marginibus involutis, abbreviatis, apice attenuatis, mucronato-acutis; paniculis laxis, nodis pilosis, spicis compositis ternatis, multifloris, pedicellis ramosis, filiformibus, flexuosis, apice incrassatis; spiculis solitariis, bifloris, sericeo-pilosis, pilis gluma duplo longioribus; gluma exteriore nulla, interioribus 2-nerviis, obtusis, dorso ciliatis; flore masculino uno, palea binervis, apice obtusa, ciliato-dentata; staminibus 3; stylis attenuatis, apice barbatis; achenio nigrescente.—*Panicum Teneriffæ*, R. Br. in Prod. i. p. 39; *Saccharum Teneriffæ*, Linn. fil. in Suppl. p. 106;

Tricholæna micrantha, Schrad. in Rœm. et Schult. Syst. Veg. Mant.
ii. p. 163; *T. leucantha*, Hochst. in Schimp. Pl. Abyss. n. 1818;
Saccharum? dissitiflorum, Edgew. Journ. Asiat. Soc. Beng. xvi. p. 1219.
Hab. Aden (*Edgew., Hook. fil. et T.* !).
Distr. In insulis Capitis Viridis ! et insulis Canariensibus ! oris Africæ
borealis ! et in insula Sicilia ! Abyssinia ! a peninsula Arabiæ usque
ad Scinde !

2. PANICUM, *Linn.*

1. P. VIRIDE (*Linn., Sp. Pl. Willd.*, i. p. 335). Radice fibroso, glabro;
culmo basi decumbente vel erecto, ligulis ciliatis; foliis lanceolatis,
acuminatis, acutis, planis, margine scabris vaginis striatis, pubescentibus; paniculis solitariis, densis, cylindricis, spiciformibus, setis scabris
asperis; setis spicula plus minus longioribus, ad basin spiculæ solitariis; spiculis sub-bifloris; glumis exterioribus obscure 4-6-nerviis,
glabris; gluma florifera (glumella) ovata, obtusa, enervi, striata, tuberculata, subcrustacea.—*Setaria viridis*, Pal. de Beauv. Agr. t. 14. f. 3.
Hab. Aden, in umbris arbuscularum (*T. Anders.*).
Distr. In toto orbe calidiore.
Annua, in Aden, herba pusilla 3-6 uncialis. *Paniculæ* interdum simplices.

3. PENNISETUM, *Pal. de Beauv.*

1. P. CENCHROIDES (*Rich. in Pers. Syn.* i. p. 72). Culmo erecto,
ramoso, glabro; vaginis glabris, margine ciliatis, ligula barbato-ciliata;
foliis linearibus, acutis, planis, pilosis; paniculis solitariis spiciformibus, cylindricis, obtusis; involucri setis aristæformibus, inæqualibus, basi plumosis, apice purpurascentibus; spiculis 2-3-floris;
gluma florifera (glumella) subcartilaginea, 3-nervia; ovario glabro;
stylis inferne connatis, plumosis.—*Cenchrus ciliaris*, Linn. Mant.
p. 320; *P. rufescens*, Spreng. in Schimp. Pl. Arab. n. 153; *Cenchrus
pennisetiformis*, Hochst. et Steud. in Schimp. Pl. Arab. n. 973; *P. ci-
liare*, Link, Hort. Ber. ii. p. 216; *P. distylum*, Guss. Fl. Sic. Prod.
Suppl. i. p. 12; *P. ciliatum*, Parlat.
Hab. Aden, in locis depressis arenosis (*Hook. fil. et T.* !).
Distr. In locis aridis regionum calidiorum Africæ et Asiæ.

Tribus STIPACEÆ.

4. ARISTIDA, *Linn.*

1. A. ADSCENSIONIS (*Linn. Sp. Pl.* p. 121). Radice fibroso, tomentoso,
culmis plurimis decumbentibus vel erectis, vaginis nodisque glabris,
ligulis obscure vel barbato-ciliatis; foliis linearibus, acutis, involutis,
margine scabris; paniculatis, coarctatis, subsecundis, basi interruptis;
spiculis unifloris; glumis subulatis inæqualibus, muticis, glabris; gluma
florifera (glumella) apice triaristata, aristis scabris.—*A. cærulescens*,

Desf. Fl. Atl. t. 21. f. 2; *A. depressa*, Retz. Obs. iv. p. 22; *A. vulgaris*, Trin. et Rupr. Stip. 131; *A. gigantea*, Linn. fil. Suppl. p. 113; *A. Canariensis*, Willd. Enum. p. 99; *A. Mauritiana*, Kunth. Gram. i. p. 265, t. 44; *A setacea*, Retz. Obs. iv. 22, in Jacq. Pl. Ind. Orient. ex Herb. Mus. Paris.; *A. Hystrix*, Roxb. Fl. Ind. ed. 1832, p. 350, fide Planchon, in herb. Hook.

Hab. Aden, rarissime (*Hook. fil. et T.*!).

Distr. Ab insulis Canariensibus per Africam borealem et centralem usque ad Ceylaniam atque Indiam orientalem.

Species variabilis, 3-uncialis vel fere 2-pedalis, plerumque glabra; nodi glabri. *Paniculæ* sæpe purpurascentes; setæ 4–6 lin. longæ, scabræ vel sublæves.

I have not given all the synonyms for this plant, but only those names that are important with reference to the flora of Arabia and India.

5. STIPAGROSTIS, *Nees.*

1. S. PLUMOSA (*Munro, MSS. in Herb. Benth.*). Cæspitosa; radice fibroso, fibris crassiusculis tomentosis; caulibus plurimis, basi vaginis marcidis vestitis, glabris, nodis constrictis, vaginis glabris apice ciliatis; foliis rigidulis, linearibus, mucronato-acutis, margine involutis; paniculis oblongis, laxis, simplicibus; ramulis capillaribus, alternis, flexuosis; pedicellis filiformibus, flexuosis, glabris, apice incrassatis; glumis inæqualibus, oblongo-lanceolatis, glabris vel puberulis, interiore exteriorem superante; gluma florifera (glumella) oblonga, involuta, tubulosa, chartacea, 3-nerva, tuberculata, longissime aristata, aristis articulatis, tortis, erectis, canaliculatis, papilloso-scabris; laciniis lateralibus barbatis, lacinia media laterales triplo quadruplo superante, plumosa; palea cuneato-obovata, apice truncata, involuta, hyalina, glaberrima.—*Aristida plumosa*, Linn. Sp Pl. p. 1666. *A. lanata*, Forsk. Descr. p. 25, *Arthratherum plumosum* in Coss. et Dur. Fl. Alg. p. 82. *A. pogonoptilum*, Jaub. et Spach, Ill. Pl. Or. iv. p. 56, t. 337. *Aristida Paradisea*, Edgew. Journ. Asiat. Soc. Bengal, vol. xvi. p. 1219.

Hab. Aden (*Edgew., Hook. fil. et T.*! *T. Anders.*).

Distr. In Arabia Felici! et Petræa! per Asiam calidam usque ad Punjab. In Abyssinia et Ægypto.

Gramen gracile et formosum. *Aristidæ ciliatæ*, Desf., proxima, sed differt foliis non abbreviatis, culmis ad nodos glabris, vaginis inconspicue ciliatis, et stipite aristæ non torto.

Tribus CHLORIDEÆ.

G. TETRAPOGON, *Desf.*

1. T. VILLOSUM (*Desf. Fl. Atl.* ii. p. 389, t. 255). Cæspitosum; radice fibroso-tomentoso; culmis paucis, erectis, basi dense vaginatis, foliatis, ad nodos glabris; vaginis striatis, glabris, rarissime infimis pilosis, supra medium margine scarioso; ligula inconspicua, non ciliata;

spicis terminalibus, solitariis, densissimis, sericeo-villosis, folio spathi-
formi involucratis; rachibus sæpe geminis, cohærentibus; spiculis
3–4-floris, longe pilosis; flosculis inferioribus hermaphroditis, superioribus sterilibus; glumis membranaceis, breviter acuminato-aristatis,
persistentibus, glabris; exteriore villosa, longe aristata, cucullata,
interiore obtusa, ciliata; gluma florifera (glumella) solitaria, villosa,
aristata.—*Chloris villosa*, Pers. Syn. i. p. 87. *C. Tetrapogon*, Pal. de
Beauv. Agrost. p. 158.

Hab. Aden! (*Hook. fil. et T.!*).

Distr. In Arabia Petræa! et Felici! Scinde! Algeria, et insulis Canariensibus!

7. DACTYLOCTENIUM, *Willd.*

1. D. ÆGYPTIACUM (*Willd. Enum.* 1029). Cæspitosum; caule prolifero
repente, radicante; culmis adscendentibus; vaginis basi tuberculatis,
pilosis, superne glabris; ligulis ciliatis; nodis constrictis, glabris; foliis
lineari-lanceolatis, acutis, planis, margine papillis piliferis sparse tuberculatis; spicis terminalibus, horizontalibus, digitatis, ternatis vel qua-
ternatis, crassiusculis, densis; rachi in mucronem prolongata; spiculis
imbricato-unilateralibus, 3–5-floris; glumis acutis marginatis, minute
ciliatis, carinatis, exteriore breviore, aristata, arista spiculis longiore;
florifera (glumella) acuta, carinata, glabra, bifida; palea carinata,
mucronata, aristata; semine transversim ruguloso.—*Cynosurus Ægyp-
tius*, Linn. Syst. Pl. p. 185. *Eleusine Ægyptiaca*, Roxb. Fl. Ind. ed.
1832, i. p. 344. *D. mucronatum* et *D. prostratum*, Willd. Enum. 1029.
D. australe, Steud. Gram. p. 212. *D. aristatum*, Link, Hort. i. p. 50.
D. Figarei, Notar. (Steud. *l. c.*). *D. distachyum*, Bojer, Hort. Maurit.
p. 370. *Chloris mucronata*, Mich. Flor. Bor.-Amer. i. p. 59.

Hab. Aden (*Hook. fil. et T.!*).

Distr. Per totum orbem calidiorem.

Tribus FESTUCACEÆ.

8. ERAGROSTIS, *Beauv.*

1. E. CILIARIS (*Link, Hort. Ber.* i. 192). Radice fibroso; culmis ramosis,
geniculatis; vaginis papilloso-tuberculatis, pubescentibus, apice ciliatis; foliis anguste linearibus, planis, patentibus; paniculis coarctatis,
thyrsiformibus, interruptis vel continuatis, compositis; spiculis 6–12-
floris; glumis membranaceis, naviculæformibus, acutis, carina bar-
bata; gluma florifera (glumella) mucronata, 3-nervi; palea ciliata.
—*Poa ciliaris*, Linn. Sp. ed. Willd. i. p. 402. *E. pulchella*, Parlat.

Hab. Aden (*T. Anders.*).

Distr. In Arabia Felici! India! et Ceylania! per totam Africam! in
insula Adscensionis! in America australi ad Para!

This is an exceedingly variable plant; my specimens from Aden are only
about 1½ inch high.

9. ÆLUROPUS, *Trin.*

1. *Æ.* ARABICUS (*Steud. Nomencl.* p. i. 30, *Gram.* p. 298). Culmis repentibus, numerosis, ramosissimis, elongatis, teretibus, incrassatis, vaginis persistentibus imbricate vestitis; vaginis margine ciliatis; ligula nulla; foliis brevissimis, rigidis, subulatis, pungenter mucronatis, glaucis; paniculis in ramis terminalibus ovatis, conglomeratis; rachi pubescente, spiculis multifloris; glumis 2, obovatis, muticis, scariosis, carinatis; gluma florifera subpatente, sericeo-ciliata, pubescente, ad apicem glabra, 3-nervi, paleam paulo superante, mucronulata; palea binervi, mucronulata vel mutico-obtusa; caryopsidibus ovatis, obtusis, glabris.—*Calotheca Arabica*, Spr. Syst. Veg. i. p. 348. *Festuca mucronata*, Forsk. Descr. p. 22. *Festuca pungens*, Vahl, Symb. i. p. 10, t. 2. *Dactylis mucronata*, Steud. Gram. p. 298.

Hab. Aden, in arenosis (*Hook. fil.!* *T. Anders.*).

Distr. In Arabia.

Cæspitosus, horridus, 2–3-pedalis. *Culmi* vaginis marcidis occulti. *Folia* glauca, ½ unc. longa. *Paniculæ* pubescentes, 1 unc. longæ.

ADDENDUM.

SINCE the printing of this *Florula*, I have seen a specimen of a *Fissenia*, collected at Aden by Dr. Courbon, of the French exploring expedition under the command of Captain Russel, and kindly communicated to Dr. Hooker for my inspection by Prof. Brongniart of Paris. This is the plant upon which Brown founded the genus, and of which I have examined his original specimen in the British Museum: it does not, however, bear the name *Fissenia*, but *Kissenia*, in honour of its discoverer, M. Kissen, a traveller in Arabia. Endlicher, who is responsible for the spelling *Fissenia*, probably obtained the generic name for the South African species, orally, from R. Brown. After a careful comparison of the Arabian and South African specimens, I can find no difference, and I therefore propose that R. Brown's name of *K. spathulata* be substituted for *F. Capensis* (and *Cnidone Mentzeloides*).

Ordo LOASACEÆ.

KISSENIA, *R. Br.* (*Fissenia*, Endl. [*errore*].)

Calycis tubus cum ovario connatus, 10-costatus; limbus 5-partitus, lobis æqualibus. *Petala* 10, decidua, in apice calycis tubi inserta; 5, calycis lobis alterna, rotunda, concava; 5, calycis lobis opposita, minora, ligulata, incurva. *Stamina* indefinita; antheris bilocularibus, introrsis. *Ovarium* triloculare; loculis uniovulatis.

1. K. SPATHULATA (*R. Br., MSS. in Herb. Mus. Brit.*). Caule erecto, striato, papillis scabris aspero; foliis alternis, petiolatis, inferioribus 3–7-lobis, superioribus lineari-lanceolatis, bracteiformibus, acutis, grosse sinuato-dentatis, utrinque asperrimis; calycis tubo ovato, in fructu 10-costato, costis pilis fulvis tomentosis; limbo 5-partito; lobis longe spathulatis, subherbaceis, 3-nerviis; petalis 10, biseriatis, calyce multo brevioribus, 5 majoribus calycis lobis alternis, carinatis, ovatis, concavis; 5 minoribus lobis oppositis, ligulatis, angulatim incurvis; stylis 3, brevibus; fructu lignoso, 3-loculari, sæpe abortu monospermo; seminibus ovatis, compressis.—*Fissenia Capensis*, Endl. Gen. Plant. Suppl. ii. p. 76, absque descriptione. *Cnidone Mentzeloides*, E. Mey. in Herb. Drège, et Presl, Bot. Bemerk. p. 73. *Fissenia Capensis*, Harvey in Thesaur. cap. i. p. 61, et t. 98, sub nomine *F. Mentzeloides*, R. Br.

Hab. Aden (*Courbon*!).

Distr. In Namaqualand, regione subtropica Africæ austro-occidentalis! *Frutex* sublignosus, asperrimus, 4–5-pedalis. *Cortex* pallidus. *Folia* 2 unc. longa, 1–1½ unc. lata; *petiolus* ½ unc. longus, teres, striatus, basi dilatatus, in nervum prominentem prolongatus. *Calyx* accrescens, in fructu 1½ unc. longus; lobis reticulato-nervatis, scabris. *Corolla* calycis lobis dimidio brevior, straminea.

INDEX.

The Synonyms are printed in Italics.

THE END.

Printed by TAYLOR and FRANCIS, Red Lion Court, Fleet Street.

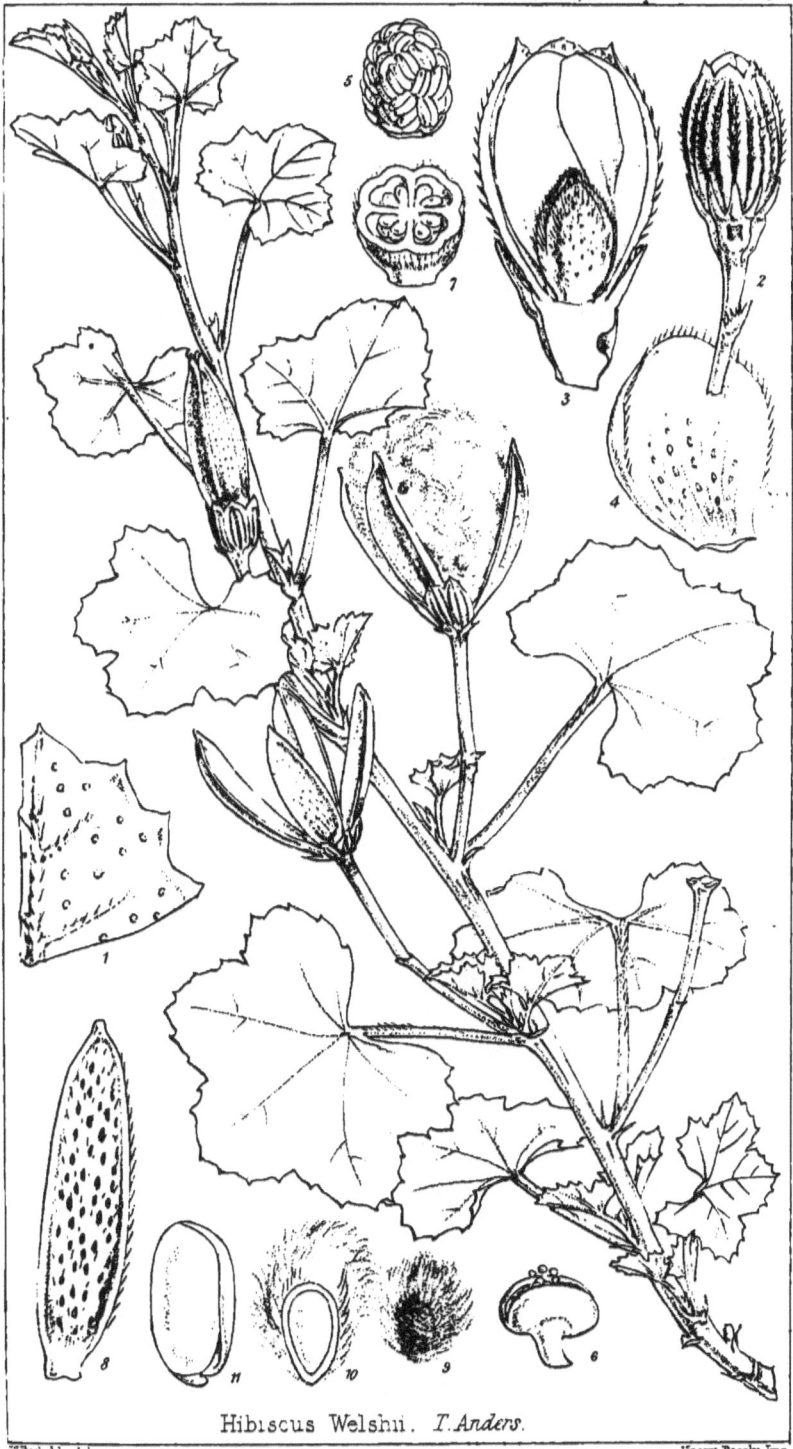

Hibiscus Welshii. *T. Anders.*

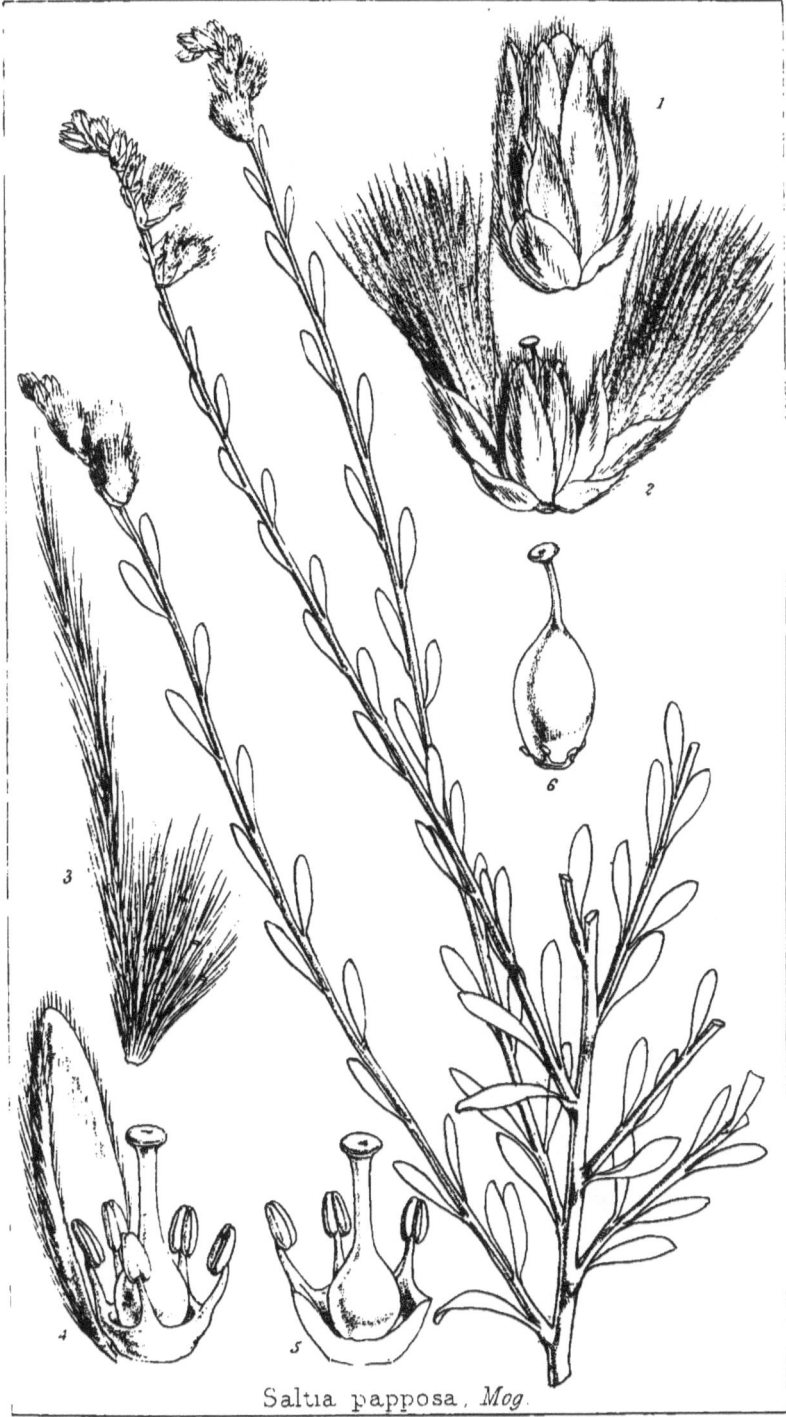

Saltia papposa, *Mog.*

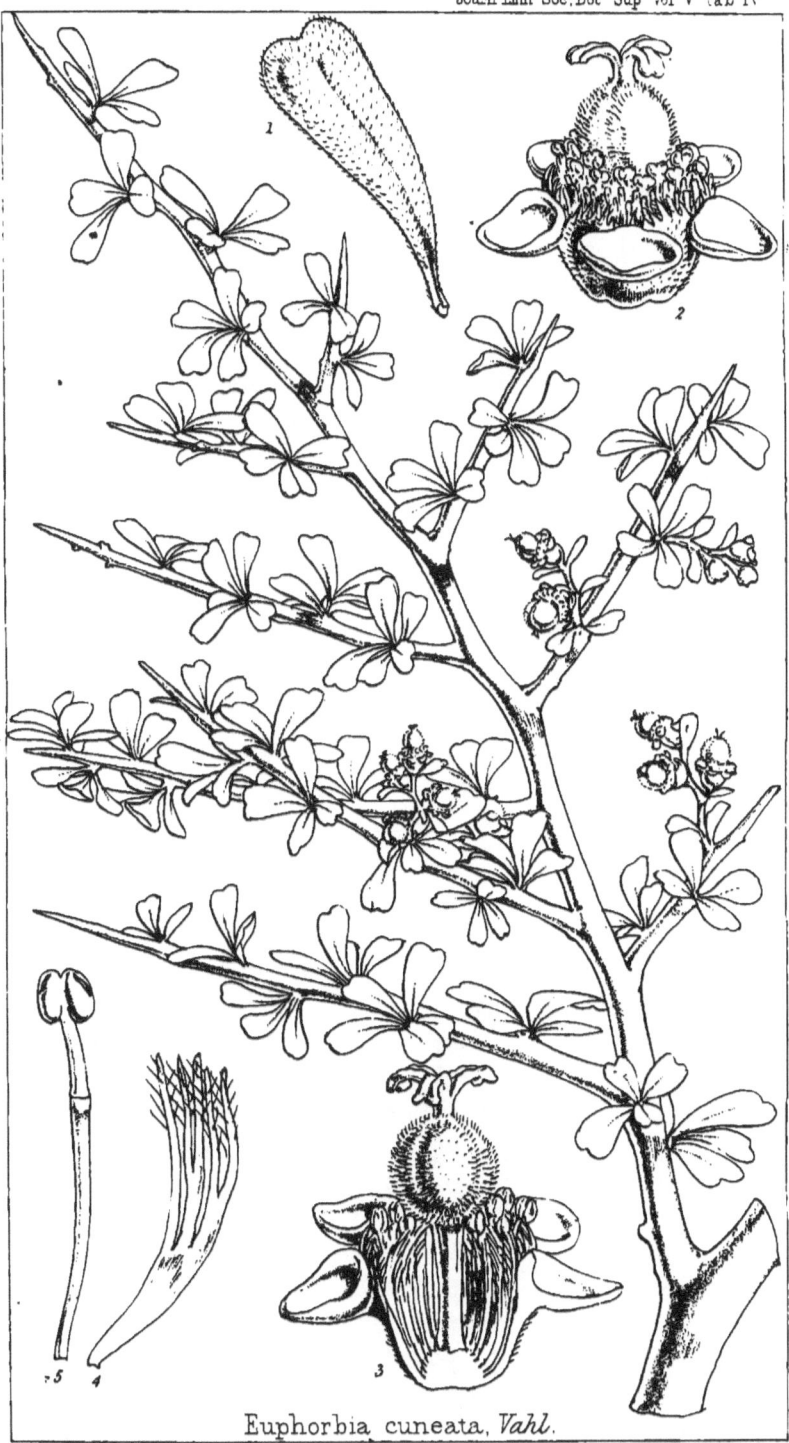

Euphorbia cuneata, *Vahl.*

W.Fitch, del et lith.

Vincent Brooks, Imp

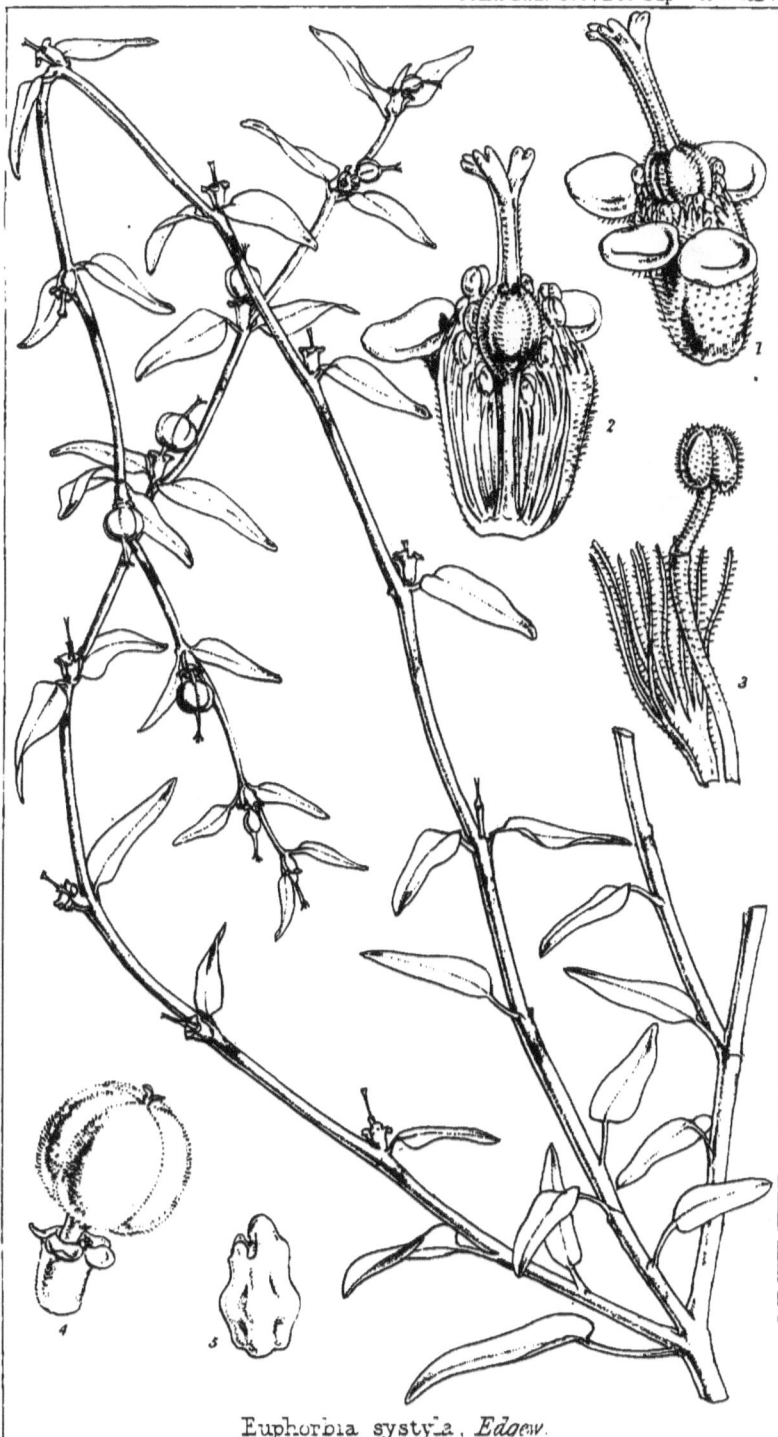

Euphorbia systyla, *Edgew.*

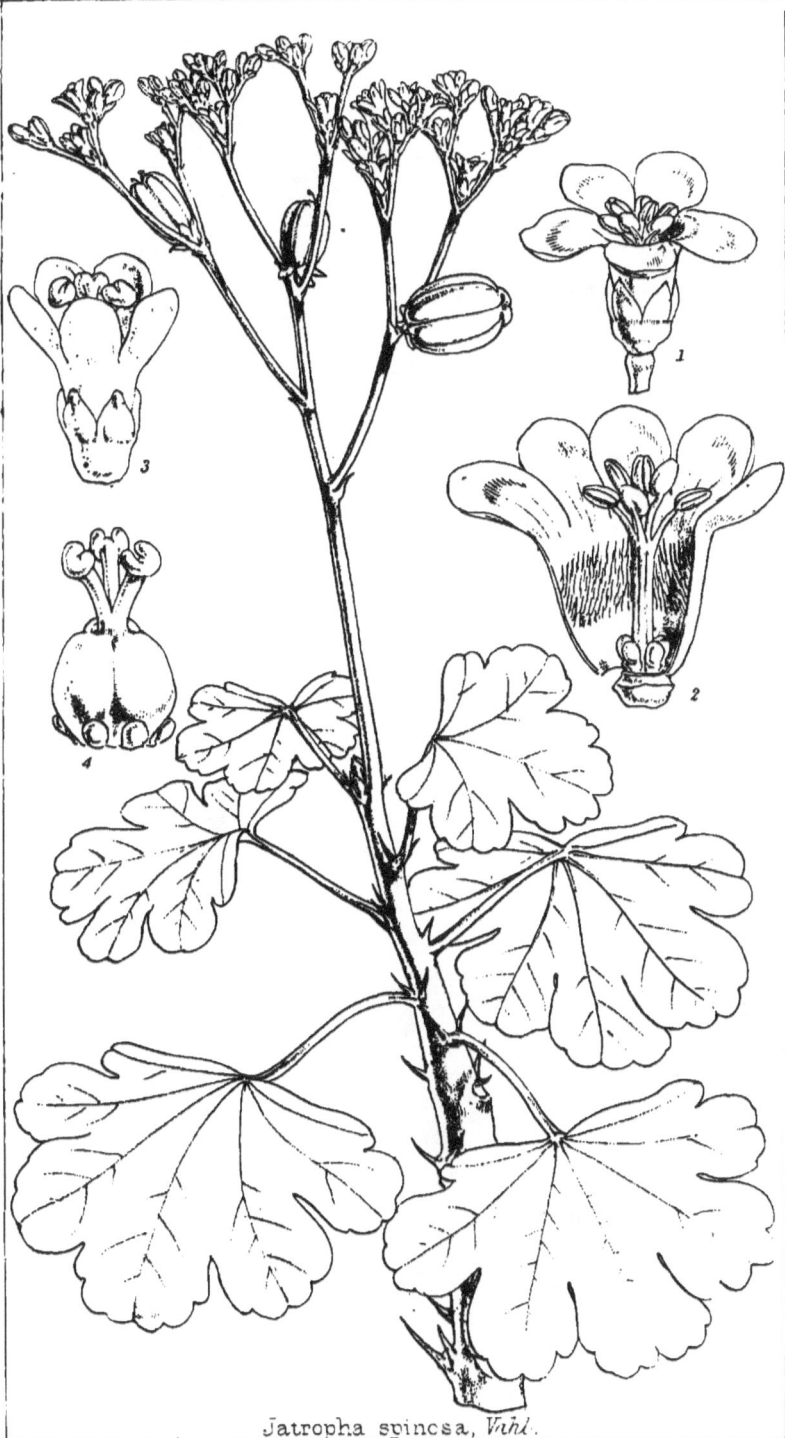

Jatropha spinosa, *Vahl*.

W. Fitch del et lith.

Vincent Brooks Imp

www.ingramcontent.com/pod-product-compliance
Lightning Source LLC
Chambersburg PA
CBHW032355020726

47499CB00008B/2766